Other titles available in the Savannah Stories:

The Savannah Stories

PAYBACK

The Savannah Stories

PAYBACK

J.L. Lemon

ISBN-13: 978-0-9909589-2-5

Published 2007
Second Edition 2015

"PFFT You Were Gone" © Susan Heather

Printed by Lulu.com in the United States of America

This book is dedicated to:

God for blessing me with the passion to write;

My family for their love, support, patience and for listening endlessly to my brainstorms;

My fifth grade English teacher, Mrs. Smith for being what teachers should be: innovative and inspiring.

Vengeance is in my heart, death in my hand,

Blood and revenge are hammering in my head.

- William Shakespeare

1

The petite brown-haired imp skipped around the playground by herself singing "It's A Small World". The last of the children had either walked home or been picked up soon after the last bell, leaving her all alone in the schoolyard.

Beneath the thick pink coat with a white fur collar, she wore a pink t-shirt declaring, "I'm the Big Sister", jeans and a pair of Keds Fairy Tale sneakers. The silver and red rhinestone charms on the toes glittered in the sun as she played hopscotch on the sidewalk.

He could recognize this child as well as her family now. He knew her habits, her food preferences, her favorite toys. She lifted her head, giving the playground another glance for her parent's car. He did the same. Seeing no one around, he slowly began the short trek to her. Little Lindsey Prince, the darling of Mrs. Grady's kindergarten class. Mostly a quiet child, Lindsey's personality blossomed outside the classroom and verged on effervescent around those she knew – and he intended to acquaint himself with her just fine.

He'd stood around the corner of the building for twenty minutes, watching her and checking his watch to ensure neither Seth or his wife arrived to pick up their daughter. After seeing Seth, he knew he never wanted to tangle with him. The burly ex-army major stood well over six feet and owned a successful self-defense studio. Women flocked to his place like swallows to Capistrano. No doubt because of his defense techniques but also his good looks. His military background still played a distinct role in his life by his demeanor and appearance but he melted like hot butter when it came to his kids. He'd avoid tackling Seth at all costs because he wasn't the target.

Seth's wife Leah worked as a nurse at Grady Hospital. She wasn't exactly hard on the eyes either and the little girl skipping around the playground was her spitting image. For weeks he'd memorized the parent's schedules until it was second nature. Today was his only chance. On Thursdays Seth worked late and his wife's shift always ran over by thirty minutes or more. Glancing one last time at his Timex, he made his decision.

He strode toward Lindsey now, calling her by name. The little girl swung around, the singing stopped. Instantly she reverted to the shy, wary youngster he'd observed for weeks. She began walking back to the school doors. He had to stop her or lose his only chance, "Your daddy sent me to pick you up, honey."

She didn't respond but kept walking. He tried mentioning her father, "You're a smart little girl. Seth taught you well not to talk to strangers but I'm a friend."

The mention of her father's name made her pause. She glanced back at him over her shoulder. He moved closer, "See, I *do* know your daddy. We were in the army together," he lied.

Still, she showed no signs of warming to him but she'd already broken one important rule Seth reminded her of every morning. *After school, stay inside the building until you see Mama's car or mine.* Maybe Lindsey would break just one more rule… "I just got back in town and he wants you and me to meet him at Aunt Georgia's house. We're all going to have pizza later."

Bingo. Lindsey's face brightened and she turned to him, "Aunt Savannah too?" He bent down to her and swept her long, dark waves behind her shoulders, "Aunt Savannah too." He had to admit the kid was cute with her turned up nose and big brown eyes that sparkled at the mention of her aunts. He knew mentioning the two women would excite her. The two spoiled Seth's kids rotten.

He noticed Lindsey's brow drew downward. She must have sensed something wrong. He was losing her and that couldn't happen. She was a means to an end for him. Once he had her, then he had Savannah – and that bitch would pay. For years he dreamed of hurting her like she had him. For months he'd meticulously planned. This year the Prince Thanksgiving table would be, at the very least, minus one person. Maybe two. When he finally trapped Savannah, he'd make sure she remembered him – just before she died. By the time he was finished with her, they'd *all* remember him.

Before dinner invitations were extended and long before Thanksgiving meal preparations, the family would place flowers on the graves of their dearly – and recently – departed loved ones. The image of it made him smile but first on his agenda was convincing little Lindsey to come with him. He gentled his voice, "You look a lot like Savannah.

Pretty as a picture with that long, dark hair and that smile."

The corners of her mouth lifted slightly as she shifted from one foot to the other, "You know Aunt Savannah too?"

He laughed, "Of course I do. Your Aunt Georgia too but Savannah was always my favorite." He congratulated himself on thinking quick. With a little more work, he'd convince Lindsey to come with him and what the hell, he might even spring for pizza after all. He tweaked the girl's nose, "So what do you say? You wanna go pig out on pizza with Daddy and your aunts?"

To his dismay, she frowned again. What did it take with this kid? Scrubbing her sneaker toes in the dirt, she sulked, "Mama won't let me eat pizza."

"Well, this is a special day and your daddy promised you can eat all you want and since Savannah's buying dinner, you don't want to hurt *her* feelings, do you?"

A definite shake of the head followed. So the kid was even closer to Savannah than he thought. He extended his hand to her, "Let's go relive the old times with Aunt Savannah. I'll make sure we have her complete and undivided attention."

Lindsey easily plopped her hand into his. Her fingers, little and warm, grasped gently at his palm, signifying acceptance. He curled his hand around hers, his voice gentle as he began her favorite song, "It's a world of laughter, a world of tears, it's a world of hopes, and a world of fears, there's so much that we share, that it's time we're aware, it's a small world after all..."

2

Savannah left work at four thirty. She and Ennis stayed through the night mulling over the latest case that stalled due to lack of evidence. They took an hour or two to doze then relied on a continuous infusion of coffee and candy bars to stoke their energy. When Georgia called early that morning to invite her to dinner, Savannah gratefully accepted. She'd invited Ennis as well but he'd begged off citing exhaustion, "I'm going home to crash and burn. Thanks for the offer though."

Now, at five thirty, and full of Southern Ham Casserole, Savannah's eyelids drooped and she battled a bout of yawning. Georgia scooped more of the casserole and angled it toward Savannah's plate.

Savannah, though, leaned back in the dining chair, patting her stomach and waving her sister off, "I'm stuffed."

Georgia prepared Savannah's favorite meal that evening and ever since the moment heavenly ham and onion wafted into her hungered senses, Savannah wondered what her sister wanted. When Georgia fixed that meal, a favor was in the works and she'd wait long enough for the food to satisfy her craving before asking.

Clearly feeling the bribe failed, Georgia sighed, "For someone who claimed starvation, you ate like a bird." To punctuate her point, she dumped the spoon into the dish with a ceremonious clank.

Blinking back disbelief, Savannah gently reminded, "I had two enormous helpings."

Georgia's left brow arched as though two helpings equated to an appetizer, "You've barely eaten since you and Ennis segregated yourselves from humanity. Staying at the station overnight isn't something I'd do often." She saw her sister preparing to defend the action and cut her off, "And if you don't eat, you'll get sick."

The finality in Georgia's tone offered no wiggle room. Offering an apologetic smile, Savannah reiterated, "I did have two helpings, Georgia. It's an excellent meal but a filling one."

Georgia always looked mistreated if the pots and pans weren't basically licked clean. It made no difference that she cooked enough for the 1st Mountain Division.

"So," Georgia began while frowning her sulkiest frown, "I suppose the chocolate cake is out of the question."

Savannah attempted to tiptoe around Georgia's feelings as best she could but her sister's Rita Hayworth features pouted like no other human possibly could, "Could I beg a piece to take home?" Georgia's hurt expression evolved to depression. Alarmed at the change, Savannah tiredly joked, "Okay, you can keep it."

Georgia still didn't smile. Now Savannah's mood sobered, "What's wrong?"

She shook her head but her younger sister didn't buy it. She asked again, marveling at Georgia's sheepish nature as she finally spilled the problem, "Want to stay the night with me again? I've really enjoyed these past few nights together and I even rented some movies we can watch. I know you're too tired tonight but maybe tomorrow night we could watch them." Since the marines recalled Matthew to the war, Georgia felt lost without someone in the house. Savannah understood the loneliness – even she missed the get-togethers she and her sister had before the marriage.

As a bonus Georgia added, "I bought some Yoo-Hoo at Kroger's today."

Georgia certainly loaded all her weapons before springing the question on her. Although she really didn't need it for a bribe, Georgia knew Yoo-Hoo was hard for her sister to turn down. A knowing smile curved Savannah's lips, "Double fudge?"

Seeing progress, Georgia allowed a smile to surface – Rita Hayworth was finally happy, "Double fudge."

Savannah's cell phone rang as she answered Georgia, "That settles it. I move in tonight." She stood to retrieve her purse and Georgia hugged her, "Thank you." The older sister barely finished speaking when her own phone began ringing.

"What is this?" Savannah exclaimed over the jangling phones, "Grand Central Station?" She grabbed her purse and glanced at the Caller ID on her cell. No number, no name – in fact, it was blocked. Not unusual but it still caught her as odd. Most people who called her didn't block their name. From the corner of her eye, she watched Georgia pick up her phone, "Hello... Hi, Seth..."

Now *that* was unusual. Seth kept to himself unless something was wrong or he needed an emergency babysitter. He did call Georgia for help with the kids so that was probably the instance this time. Savannah clicked on her phone, "Prince,"

"Don't make me wait again." The command came from a male voice.

At first Savannah figured it for a wrong number since she didn't recognize the voice. Still, whoever the creep was, he shouldn't be so rude, "Obviously you've got the wrong number."

"Obviously you need to learn who's in charge right now," he taunted.

Her fingers wearily combed her long hair. She just wanted to end this absurd conversation and go to bed, "Who is this?" In the lull of her strange conversation, she heard Georgia on the phone with their brother. That's when fatigue took a backseat. The stress in Georgia's voice was crystal clear, "Seth, calm down. She's on her phone right now, that's why you couldn't get through."

Savannah knew by Georgia's tone something was very wrong. Normally Seth and Georgia could get along on the phone but something had them both flustered. Judging by Georgia's voice, he must be panicked. Savannah wanted off the phone. "Who is this?" she asked again, her voice insistent. "Tell me now or I hang up." Again, there was no answer. Fed up with the prank and wanting to turn her attention to Seth, she palmed the phone to disconnect... Then she heard a voice, faint at first then louder. The terrified voice of her niece, "Aunt Savannah?"

Adrenaline flooded her, bringing her wide awake. The phone

raced back to her ear, "Lindsey?"

The little girl was crying, her words scarcely understandable, "Help me. He's going to hurt me if you don't."

Savannah steadied herself against the dining table. She willed her heart to stop pounding in her throat and chest. Her mind refused to accept the obvious. A stranger had Lindsey. God only knew for how long and what he'd already done to her. All she knew for sure was Lindsey's fear was palpable and real. The child was scared to death. Savannah tried to eradicate her own fear from her voice, "Honey, are you alright?"

She sniffed back her tears, managing, "I'm scared."

"I know, honey, just try to stay calm. Do you recognize the man you're with?"

"No," was the trembling reply. Her crying again escalated from sniffling to outright breathless sobbing, "Come get me, Aunt Savannah. *Please...*"

It sliced Savannah to the soul to hear the girl pleading hysterically, to hear the terrified weeping. Retaining any shred of control took a monumental effort, "Sweetheart, calm down." She leaned toward Georgia and pointed to the phone. "I'm coming for you," she said, hoping to allay Lindsey's fears if even a little. "Tell me if you recognize where –"

The next voice was adult and very male, "You're in for a long journey so save your breath. You will do everything I say and follow my instructions to the letter or I'll make sure you regret not doing so. Do not push me, Savannah, or else..." there was a silence then Lindsey suddenly cried out.

Savannah's temper boiled inside, her fingers gripped the dining table with such force dishes rattled and glasses threatened to fall over. Georgia watched her from across the room and quietly spoke to Seth. Savannah couldn't restrain her anger any longer, "You touch her again and I'll serve *you* to the lions in the zoo – *in very small pieces.*"

Georgia's conversation halted. She mumbled something to Seth but still kept an eye on her sister.

The man laughed at Savannah's flare-up, "Still got that temper, don't you? If you want to save your niece, look under your car's windshield wiper." His voice dropped to an unsettling hush, "And don't worry about us. Lindsey and I will have fun together. I'm *real* good with little girls and she's just *darling.*"

"I swear if you hurt her –" Savannah growled but the phone went dead, cutting off the rest of her threat. Her thumb jabbed the "off" button, she glanced at her sister then headed for the door. She raced outside, hearing Georgia cut Seth's call short as well. Despite the approaching dusk, when Savannah reached her car she clearly saw a note pinned down by the wiper, its edge flapping in the wind. The cold air chilled her, making her shiver from not only cold but anxiety. She unfolded the note just as Georgia rounded the front fender, her long waves taking a beating from the swift breeze. She brushed a few wayward curls from her eyes and crossed her arms for warmth, "Seth is beside himself. He said this guy called him and said not to contact anyone but you. He hasn't even asked for money yet. What do you think that means?"

She honestly didn't want to think about it, "How the hell would I know? I only know he told me to come out here for this." The two read the typewritten note together, "You will not notify the authorities. If you do, I'll kill her but I'll have my fill of her first and I'll tell her it's your fault she's suffering. Her mama and daddy will never forgive you, Savannah. I'll send them reminders of their daughter's misery, of her last moments. They won't have a minute's peace and neither will you. What you *will* do: You will follow my instructions in a timely manner or Lindsey will suffer from your incompetence. There is a cell phone in your front seat. Take it. Give your other cell phone to your sister. She is not to notify anyone of this situation. If you, Georgia or Seth violate my rules, the girl dies. With the phone you'll find an envelope with additional instructions in your car. Remember, time is precious, especially if you're Lindsey."

Savannah cursed aloud. The word bitterly fell from her lips and temporarily stunned her sister. Georgia, however, regrouped quickly, "I suppose you don't know who –"

"No, I don't," she answered abruptly. "But once I find out, I'll kill the bastard and I don't care if I lose my shield because of it. *I'll kill him.*"

"Well, he knows our names so he's not a stranger."

An insistent chime broke the silence – the cell phone in the car rang again. Savannah fumbled with the door handle and palmed the phone in seconds. It was him, "Have you discarded your other phone yet? And have you read the note?"

"No and no. You didn't give me much time."

"You have five minutes and the clock starts."

The caller hung up, leaving her and Georgia staring cluelessly at each other. Checking her watch once more, she scrambled to find the instructions. The glowing dome light revealed no envelope. It wasn't in plain sight – nothing on the dashboard or in the seat. Panic set in, "Help me find an envelope. It has instructions in it. He gave me five minutes to find it."

Georgia sprang into action. While Savannah dug through her suit jacket laid across the seat, Georgia rounded the passenger's side, opened the door and searched under the seats, "Why would he hide it? Most kidnappers want money and fast. They don't send people on perverse scavenger hunts."

Savannah pushed the driver's seat forward and burrowed to the back seat. If she had to tear the Camaro apart to find it, she would. Jamming her hands in the crevice between the seat and back, she dug deep, hoping evidence of an envelope, slip of paper, anything. Instead, the search became futile, "Don't know and don't care right now. Just find the damn envelope. Try the glove compartment." But somehow she *did* know. This man made the abduction personal to her and she had a feeling he wanted her to panic, to barely squeak by on time just to reinforce his power and control over her.

Georgia moved to the glove compartment, shoved papers and flashlights aside. Savannah heard papers shuffling while Georgia flipped through them, "I found it," she said a few seconds later. She handed it between the seats to Savannah.

She glanced at the typewritten name, "To: Detective Savannah

Prince" Savannah's hands shook while trying to rip it open. It wasn't the time to fall apart, she told herself but her fingers refused to cooperate. She'd never reacted like this on a case – but it hadn't been personal before.

Georgia covered her hand with hers, her voice composed, "Let me open it."

She looked at her watch again. Three minutes had passed, "He knows me personally. Who the hell could it be?"

"Calm down, Savannah. He's a freak," the hard emphasis on the last word was punctuated with a ripping sound. Georgia's thumbnail sliced the envelope open, "You can only deal with freaks if you keep your head about you." She cleared her throat and began to read the note aloud, "The one distinct feature I recall about you is your dark sense of humor. Let's play a game to see if you remember me. Who, according to you, should be spayed or neutered by a veterinarian to stop them from reproducing?" Confused, Georgia's brow sank and she looked at her sister.

"Child molesters," Savannah sounded defensive. "But I've said it a million times to a thousand people, all of whom agreed with me."

"Obviously one didn't."

"Oh, come on," she griped back. "Do you know how many of those assholes I've put away over the years? None of them exactly promised to send flowers. Now I can't even call Ennis to find which ones were paroled lately."

"I know," Georgia agreed then continued reading. "There's a place not Pharr from here where children play and have fun. Its history is tainted – many years ago the KKK roamed freely here. It once had the name of a businessman, later the name of a cop. Go where the tombstones rise above the earth, look to the northeastern side for the name P. K. Brown. There you'll find the next clue. You have 45 minutes to find it."

Savannah grabbed the note, re-read it and shook her head, "What is he talking about?"

"Wait. Let's think about it," Georgia's eyes closed to concentrate. "Pharr Road runs through Buckhead. A history of the KKK..." She shook her head, shrugging, "A businessman and a cop."

Savannah pondered aloud, "A park and a cemetery..."

As her sister seemed lost, so was Georgia. But as the moments passed, it dawned on Georgia, "KKK and a businessman. Cemetery has to be close to the park..." Her eyes widened, "Bagley Park in Buckhead! There's a black cemetery there. That's what he's talking about. They renamed it in the early eighties to Frankie Allen Park. Frankie Allen was the cop."

"I should have paid more attention in history class, obviously. Frankie Allen –" she was interrupted by the phone. "What?" she snapped at him.

"Your time starts now," he said and hung up.

"I gotta go," she told Georgia. "If you hear from Seth, tell him I'll get Lindsey back then I'll kill the bastard who took her."

3

A traffic jam along Peachtree shaved ten minutes off the forty-five minute window to Frankie Allen Park. Savannah swerved and cut between cars, driving as fast as traffic allowed and ignoring the honking horns of angry drivers.

With five minutes to spare, she brought the Camaro to a screeching halt in the northeast parking lot of Frankie Allen Park. With flashlight in hand, she sprinted through the grass toward a shelter of trees ahead. The sight of all the monuments disheartened and frustrated her, forcing her to ask for help finding the name on the note. Seeing her panic, a young man offered to search with her. After having the note in hand, she labored over its meaning. The light illuminating the words only revealed more confusion for Savannah, not answers.

"Heaven, Hell or Purgatory – where shall you go? I'm sending you to Hell, Savannah. There you will search for the next set of instructions. No Milling about – this particular Trinity will hopefully bring Liberty to your niece but only if you work fast. You have 25 minutes to complete this task." Savannah stared, stunned. He'd given her a riddle of all things – and, of course, she sucked at riddles.

Once in her car, she dialed Georgia, knowing she was the puzzle solver of the family. "Help me with this," she implored, trying to catch her breath. She threw the Camaro in reverse and rattled off the note only to hear silence in return.

"Heaven, Hell or Purgatory?" The trio of names stumped her sister as well. "Sounds like a revival of some kind."

"Listen again," Savannah read it as she entered the freeway headed south.

Georgia groaned, "I don't know. It's a weird sounding note. 'No milling about'?"

"It's capitalized. Mill, like a stone mill or something. And the word 'Liberty' is also capitalized."

"Of course!" Her sister cried elated, "The Tribulation Nightclub moved into an old mill on Liberty Avenue. They have three nightclubs there – Heaven, Hell and Purgatory. Take Northeast Parkway and turn left onto Liberty Avenue. The nightclub is at the bottom of a hill."

"Go there often, do you?" Savannah inquired with a noticeable lilt.

"I've been to Heaven a few times, Hell only once and that was enough. A friend took me but she's more gung ho about Hell's Saturday nights than anyone I've seen. Why would he send you there?"

"Your guess is as good as mine." It took fifteen minutes to arrive at the Romanesque–style building. In her entire career, she'd never been to Tribulation. She assumed the establishment kept a pretty clean reputation since the police weren't forced to frequent it. Despite the three peculiar named levels, she figured she'd walk into a normal everyday nightclub. When she drove up, she had no reason to believe otherwise.

On the outdoor marquee, "Tribulation" was spelled in purple neon script. Below the neon was a sign highlighting the week's events. A local techno band played in Heaven's section and… Then Savannah did a doubletake. Making sure to take one pertinent letter after another, she found reading it a second time as mind-boggling as the first. Stupefied, she heard herself mumble, "Tonight in Hell. Rope Bondage." Below that ad was another announcing that every Saturday in Hell was "Sin Night – Where your most erotic fantasies and worst nightmares are brought to life." *Rope bondage and erotic fantasies. Welcome to your own hell, Savannah…* Suddenly she couldn't imagine Georgia consorting with anyone interested – much less involved – in the BDSM lifestyle. Most people kept it under wraps, at least with the general public.

On a whim, she dialed Georgia again, "Find another friend."

"What are you talking about?"

"That friend that dragged you to Hell? Did you have to bring your own whips and chains too? I wouldn't drag my worst enemy here unless my purpose was to torture them. Do you realize what Saturday night *means* in this place?"

"It's Sin Night. Why?" Then her sister's meaning slowly dawned on Georgia, "For God's sake, Savannah. It was one time and no, I did not participate. Now get your mind out of the gutter and tell me what the next note says."

"Don't know yet. I'm just now entering Hell's Half Acre. I'm just glad I missed Norman Bates Night on Halloween." Then she tossed in a joke, "Oh, in case you're interested, tonight's Rope Bondage Night." She heard Georgia's exasperated grumble before hanging up. She pocketed the cell phone and opened the door. A man strode by and she waved him down, "I need directions to Hell, please. I'm sure it's in the general direction of down but how do I get there?"

The mid-twenties young man dressed in blue jeans and worn rust colored t-shirt scanned her attire then crooked his mouth, perplexed, "You sure Hell is where you want to go?"

A weak smile surfaced, "I'm sure it's *not* where I want to go. However I was instructed to go there and don't think the guy meant it exclusively as a metaphor."

He shrugged then pointed across the room at a stairway to the basement, "Good luck," he offered. She didn't like the way it sounded either. Savannah could hear the music already. Iron Butterfly's "In-A-Gadda-Da-Vida" played beneath her, the bass line and drums throbbing against her feet. She'd always hated the song – it sounded too deranged. Plus, it invoked images of drugs and free sex, just another reason it unnerved her. The closer she got to the basement entrance, the clearer the words and music became.

Savannah fortified her resolve, took a deep breath and started her journey to Hell. Taking a cursory glance downstairs, she saw streaks of purple and pink lights sweeping the darkness. *It's nothing more than a damn disco*, she tried to assure herself. Then a nagging doubt arose. *Why didn't that guy act like it was a disco?* She couldn't stifle the slight uncomfortable feeling rolling in the pit of her stomach. Something wasn't right about naming a place Hell, she kept thinking. Not unless it *really* meant it...

Taking a deep breath, she started down the stairs. A hand on her arm stopped her, "Cover charge, babe. Five bucks."

The weak smile emerged again as she reached in her pocket for the money. In the revolving lights, he caught a glimpse of the badge on her belt and withdrew his hand, "Free entrance to Hell for Atlanta's Finest. Be my guest."

She wasn't sure how to take that statement. Being told to go to Hell was one thing but when someone smiled when they said it...

On her way down the stairs, the music came into full range, as did the purple and pink lights flashing and spinning from a DJ's stage. Then it all culminated: the outdoor marquee, rope bondage, the name Hell *and* her mounting nausea. Suddenly she felt saturated in Atlanta's underworld. The clientele dressed in leather and bondage gear. Some women danced in nothing but leather thongs, pasties and studded dog collars. Others dressed in skintight leather from head to toe. Others in corners were busy with activities Savannah felt should be outlawed, especially in public. It took all she had not to turn, run and not look back.

"You're a newbie to the scene, I can tell," a man said from behind her. *No, I'm more like a Never-bie,* she wanted to say. His voice deepened as he leaned closer, "What's your pleasure, sweetheart? I aim to please charming little pets like you."

Savannah wheeled around to face what amounted to a Redwood with arms. Broad shoulders, biceps as big as barrels and a well-muscled chest eclipsed her while what amounted to a leather ski mask concealed his identity.   His other attire – Savannah used the term loosely – consisted of leather pants, gloves and a leather vest. *Perfect pervert wear*, she thought.

"Thanks for the offer but I formally decline," she answered. He stepped nearer, eliminating the space between them *and* her comfort level. She nearly gave him an up close and personal look at her badge – slammed against his nose. He smiled behind the leather hood, "Don't be shy, love. We all have to be new at some point. I'm very gentle and patient with my first-timers."

"And I'm sure they're grateful for it." By now her tolerance wore thin, "Listen, I'm running late –"

"Are you sure you're not interested in my offer, Detective Prince?"

Surprised by the calling of her name, Savannah's blue eyes rose to meet his again while her mind forewarned her to be careful. He was an accomplice of sorts, whether willing and knowledgeable about the situation or just foolishly lured to participate by a psycho.

She focused on his features, the few visible ones. His eyes were dark, nearly black and when he smiled, his teeth were perfectly aligned and perfectly white. "I'm here for a note," she replied. "Do you have it because it's very important I read it now."

He nodded once, confident in his position over her, "You will have to earn it, however. I was told you would comply with my wishes for one hour."

Savannah's temper rose then leveled out. This was no time to lose her composure, "Who told you this?"

"I was instructed not to say." His gloved hand stroked her cheek, "Come now, love. Follow me."

Containing her rage always proved difficult for her, especially when someone felt free to command her every move. Her nails dug into her palms when she fisted her hands and tilted from his touch, "I don't participate in this lifestyle and if I did, submissive is *not* my role."

His arrogant laugh caused Savannah to take a deep, calming breath. She needed a way out of this. Several people passed by, giving them a second glance. The man grew incensed with the delay, particularly when a dominatrix sidled up behind Savannah and smiled, "Got a tough one, don't you, Master Rob?" She leaned in, "Give her to me and I'll tame her for you."

"I'll tame her just fine," he snapped. "Go find your own sub. This one's mine."

The dominatrix petted Savannah's long hair, "I don't know. This one's got spirit. Made just for me." She whispered in Savannah's ear, "We'll have fun together, sweetheart." She punctuated the remark with a slap to Savannah's behind.

Savannah stiffened and turned with a glare, making quite sure the dominatrix viewed her badge. The woman stepped back, apologizing profusely.

Master Rob took Savannah by the arm, claiming her before any other intruders came around, "My contact informed me you weren't a submissive. He also said you were desperate to win a prize that he possessed. Now, how badly do you want this prize, Detective?"

She stared into the blackness of his eyes, knowing there was really only one answer. "Where do we go?"

He smiled again. The grasp on her arm tightened as he led her through the crowd. They snaked in and out of small groups talking, other groups dancing, and others in the midst of activities she feared awaited her. *You're a certified fool*, she berated herself. If Lindsey's life didn't hang in the balance, she'd never have agreed to go with him. Furthermore, he'd not be standing and absolutely not be *smiling* at her.

They angled off behind the DJ's stage and into a quieter portion of the club. The place still had plenty of industrial ambience with giant pulleys and wheels, gray stone walls and massive timber supports stretching above her. Once past the nightclub, the building mostly reverted back to its original design which didn't console Savannah in the least. They headed toward the back of the mill where no one lingered. She heard no voices, no movement. They were alone in this part of the building as they veered down a smaller, dimly lit hallway. Tugging her along, he directed, "You address me as Master and you'll follow my orders or pay with pain. Do you understand?"

Savannah would have answered but she couldn't unclench her jaw. The alarm and anger finally built to the point of no return. Only a muted "M-hmm" surfaced.

Master Rob abruptly stopped. His grasp on her arm hardened again, "Address me correctly."

She implored her jaw to slacken. As her mouth opened, her jaw trembled from the sheer power she'd exerted on the joint. *Yes, Master Asshole, I understand.* She trapped the words behind pursed lips and switched it out for the more appropriate, "Yes, Master." Luckily she forced the words without heaving as her stomach yearned to do.

He tugged her further down the hall to an open door. He flipped on the light and shut the door behind them. Savannah scanned the shadowy room then swallowed hard. This guy was hardcore into the lifestyle. The small bed had no sheets but thick leather four-point restraints. Bolted restraints adorned the blood red walls. A cabinet across the room gave her more than pause. A full length bullwhip, a flogger, riding crop and other BDSM instruments met her vision. She refused to look anymore for her gut churned like a spring storm inside her. If she continued her perusal of the room, Georgia's casserole would end up the new wall treatment. Whoever had Lindsey knew this equaled bottom-feeding to Savannah.

Master Rob's hand eased down her back, "Turn around."

She did. When she faced him, his smile widened, "Take off your clothes."

Driven to the edge of uncontrolled rage, Savannah didn't verbally refuse. Swallowing became impossible. She couldn't even move without threat of violence toward this… this so-called male of the species. She didn't trust herself not to hurt him but she'd be damned if he'd hurt *her*.

His eyes narrowed, "Take 'em off." His large hand reached toward her blouse to begin the process of undressing her.

Her mouth curled into a snarl and she tore his hand away. Keeping a solid grip, she twisted his arm behind him and slammed her foot against the back of his knee, dropping him to the floor with a solid grunt emanating from his powerful form. Surprised but still maintaining a shred of optimism, he attempted to persuade her, "Look, lady. You haven't even seen what I can do. Give me fifteen minutes and I promise you'll want more."

She straddled his legs but kept one knee in his back while reaching for her handcuffs, "If I ever sink to that level of indignity, I'd expect my family to commit me. Hands behind your back." When he didn't comply, Savannah clutched the hood and yanked his head back, "Having problems understanding me? I'll make it simple. Either do what I say or I'll hurt you and I don't mean in a nice way."

He struggled beneath her, trying to throw off her balance. His massive arms began pushing him onto his knees. Annoyed with his outright defiance, Savannah's fingers wrapped harder in the hood and shoved her other fist into his kidney, giving it a solid blow.

He sank flat against the floor with a capitulating groan then reached behind him. Locking one wrist in, she listened to him protest, "This is really unnecessary. I sorta get that you don't want to participate."

"On the contrary, *Master*," she locked his other hand behind him. "I'm definitely in the mood now." The comment didn't set well with him and she fiercely fought to stay astride the writhing leather-clad mammoth. The fight intensified when she unzipped the hood and removed it. Had anyone interrupted them, she would have felt odd but she also figured their struggle wouldn't raise eyebrows with the BDSM crowd. In fact, they'd probably stick around to watch.

He turned away to prevent her from seeing his face until she pushed his cheek to the floor, "Well, Master Rob, seems the tables have turned. You just lie here like a good little boy while I take a look around." She pushed to her feet and approached the nearby cabinet. She opened a drawer teeming with a vast assortment of toys and restraints. A repulsed sneer crept across her face. She wished for a pair of latex gloves but settled for a tissue from a Kleenex box. Various motorized gadgets were shoved aside – she didn't want to know where they'd been but had a good idea and instinctively grabbed another tissue, "And to think our ancestors must have been thoroughly bored with their sex lives."

"You'd be surprised how arousing those can be. If you'd unlock-"

"If a guy came at me with *these*," she lifted a small chain with a pair of alligator clips attached to both ends, "he'd slink away wearing 'em on the family jewels."

He winced at the description then complained, "You know, you have no right to treat me like this. In fact, I could tell this guy what you did and you won't get the prize you wanted."

The words set her temper ablaze. He would do it and Lindsey would die. Savannah pocketed the chain and reached in the drawer. Scrounging, she realized this was Master Rob's personal effects. After additional rummaging, she ran across a small gold nugget, "You'd better think twice about that, Robert Patrick Avery of Sable Run Road."

The sound of his name and address brought his face around to her. She waved his driver's license back and forth as she neared him. Bending down to him, she took a fistful of his thick, black hair and lifted his gaze to hers, "Listen carefully. I know your face, I know your name and where you live. Being that I'm a police officer, I can *and will* come to your house, raid your little dungeon, repossess all your sex toys and post your face on the department website as a sexual threat to society – if you do not tell this freak I played your stupid game. Got it?"

Avery grimaced at the tight hold. His hesitancy spurred her harder and she displayed two pictures of his children, "You'd rather these darlings find out Daddy dresses like a freak and preys on the female population rather than getting it at home with Mommy?" She gave another tug on his hair, "You *will* regret tangling with me, I promise. He's got someone very dear to me and I'm not above committing murder right now. Considering I have one hour and all these delightful instruments, I can make life a genuine pain." She withdrew the chain and dangled the alligator clips in front of his nose, "Since I can't find him but I do have *you*, guess who the recipient of my pent-up rage is?"

"Okay, *okay*," he finally agreed. "He said he'd call."

"Who is he? I want a name."

Again he flinched at the pressure she used, "He didn't tell me. He approached me in the club the other night. He handed me two thousand dollars, an envelope, a picture of you and told me what to do. He was dressed like I was, you know, a mask. I couldn't even tell you what he looks like."

She nearly swallowed her tongue, "Two thousand dollars for one hour?"

"My fee plus a bonus. He told me you wouldn't go easily and since you were a cop I wasn't about to approach you for no five hundred. Especially with what he wanted me to do. I told him I'd do it but I wasn't going to, I swear."

"Aren't you the chivalrous one. You'd better lie convincingly again to him or you'll have me breathing down your neck and you won't like it."

"I'll tell him you were an angel, does that work?"

"Just tell him I followed through," she let him go. "I haven't been called an angel since I wore diapers."

He groaned, "Can't imagine why."

"Want me to test my aim with that bullwhip?"

He vehemently shook his head. She searched the cabinet drawers for a note and finally found her name typed on the front, "I assume this is the note I'm supposed to get."

Avery nodded. She opened it and read silently, "Go to 5200 Piedmont and locate the book 'Up All Night' in fiction because you will be up all night. Between its pages you will find your next instructions. I've decided you should learn a lesson in humility and I trust the Master provided a thorough introductory course. You have only 20 minutes to discover the next clue." Savannah folded the note and pocketed it.

Avery glanced at her, "You know, you're better than the last dominatrix I visited. Have you ever thought about –"

She scowled at him, "One more word and I'm liable to test drive every one of those implements on you. Simultaneously."

4

The Camaro came to a halt a mere inch from the curb. Savannah slammed the door hard, generously rocking the car and headed in the direction of 5200 Piedmont. The angle parking along Piedmont presented a hazard unto itself. The sheer amount of traffic forced her to park halfway down the block – yet another delay in time.

She tilted her watch toward a street lamp. It read 10:00. She had to hustle if she intended to get the next clue. Extra time would help her think. The man purposefully kept her on the run so she'd tire out and *not* have time to analyze the situation. While at Tribulation, she tried to analyze who held a personal grudge against her but Avery made it impossible to think, rambling about how his family couldn't find out, how his career would kamikaze once his colleagues discovered his lifestyle. Finally she told him to shut up, that dentists were always labeled as sadists.

As she took note of the street numbers, images of Lindsey filled her mind, each worse than the last. God only knew what the man did or was doing to her.

Savannah's stride increased to a jog but before she realized it, she'd slowed to a frustrating gait that, she was convinced, even a crippled turtle could outpace. Weaving through the crowd, Savannah found it hard to believe Atlanta's pulse throbbed this intense at night. Dozens of people gathered at the café ahead – some inside, some sitting outside in wrought iron chairs. The bars along the street teemed with humanity, either tipsy or blind, staggering drunk. The closer she got to the café, the more congested the population became.

A sudden grasp on her arm stopped her meager progress and she spun, an expression of pure molten fire scorched the offender, sending him back a step, "Whoa, sugar, don't bite. I'm an ally, remember?"

Without acknowledging the comment, she began her sprint again, talking as she ran, "Ennis, go home."

Her partner picked up the pace alongside her, "What's going on? We've had calls about a runaway Camaro all over the city. When Josh got the license number, he knew something was wrong since you never drive that recklessly. Now tell me."

"I can't. Now please go." She continued to shrug past people, slide between others and she sincerely debated displaying her badge and ordering everyone to get the hell out of her way. But now she had a new obstacle to overcome: Ennis. And he wasn't letting her out of his sight.

She tried to outrun him – or at the very least outmaneuver him to lose him in the throng of people – but his powerful legs made the effort futile. Instead, he grabbed her arm, spun her again and planted his lips on hers. Instinctively, Savannah's hands shoved against his shoulders to break the kiss. Ennis held tight and even forced her backward until she stood flush against the brick wall of the café behind them.

The kiss briefly stunned her. Sheer need seemed to drive Ennis momentarily, as though finally finding her released a mounting desire for this kiss. He'd never taken such blatant liberties with her in the months since they partnered up. They kissed but not… like… this… He was a free spirit – a damn handsome one – but also tended toward the chauvinistic side, especially if he saw a woman in trouble. His steady hold on her revealed his protective nature. He possessed a sincere yearning to help her, to learn what was wrong – or he wouldn't release her at all.

Settling into the kiss so Ennis might back off, Savannah gradually opened her eyes. His overbearing action, albeit unsolicited, calmed her somewhat, at least enough to realize he'd dragged himself from bed to find her. His attire of jeans, dark blue t-shirt shirt and a Dallas Cowboys jacket appeared hurriedly thrown on. Even his coffee brown hair waved in a wild tousled manner that begged her to smooth it into place.

As the kiss progressed, people momentarily stopped, others lifted a brow but all went about their business seconds later. Savannah felt his fingers tighten around her arms and his body settle against hers – no doubt pinning her from escape – then felt his kiss lose its urgency. He parted from the devouring lip-lock but remained close enough his lips brushed hers, "You scared the hell out of me. You're gonna kill yourself driving like that."

After a moment, she finally realized what he meant, "You were following me?"

Her tone backed him off but not enough for her to entertain a possible escape. "Since Glen Iris Drive, yeah." He took a deep breath, paused, then before saying something he'd regret, dove in for another kiss, this one more unyielding than the last. It was also shorter, "What's making you this crazy?"

"I told you –"

He gently shook her, "Let me help you, Savannah. You're scared to death and that's scaring *me*."

She glanced at her watch. Five minutes to spare. A ringing drew her attention away from Ennis, "I have to get this." She answered the phone to hear the same familiar voice, "Shame, shame for breaking the rules already. I'm disappointed but not nearly as much as Lindsey will be."

The air left her lungs and her knees nearly buckled. If Ennis hadn't pinned her against the wall, she would have collapsed. Feeling her body slacken, he reinforced his grasp. Her partner watched her search the people passing by. His brow sank as he tried to follow her line of vision.

Savannah fought to regain her composure. The nutcase was watching her closely and she hadn't known it until now, "No, I haven't. I don't know how he found me." She lowered her voice to a whisper, "But I didn't contact him."

His tone chilled her, "I'm giving you the benefit of the doubt this time. Get rid of him, Savannah. Your partner's presence is jeopardizing the trust I thought we had together. The longer he hangs around, the more I'm convinced you want to break it. You have an appointment to keep so get busy."

The line went dead. She stood, staring blankly into Ennis's chest.

She wanted to cry. The urge hadn't been so overwhelming in years. Tears gathered but reality forced her to sniff them back. Holding herself together remained vital. Showing any sign of weakness gave the freak more power over her but Ennis's hold comforted her, reassured her he was there for her – if she would only speak up. She could easily get used to the idea, not to mention the feeling of his embrace.

Ennis lowered his head until they met eye to eye, "Tell me what's going on or I follow you and I have a feeling that's the last thing you want." When she didn't speak up, he continued, "Whoever that was just sapped the life out of you. You're shaking, for God's sake."

She hadn't noticed until he mentioned it but her body was trembling in his hold. From head to toe she was drained of more than mere energy. Hope began to wane too. Since the kidnapper saw her partner approach, she could pray Lindsey stayed safe long enough for her to save her. Savannah felt Ennis's grasp tighten again, the pressure lifted her vision to his.

His eyes held a distinct message – he meant to find out somehow and the choice was hers. She desperately wanted to tell him. She needed to share with someone besides her family and she trusted Ennis implicitly. His easygoing boyish side she'd grown accustomed to evolved to a poise he developed for ferreting out the truth. He physically closed in on her, pressuring her to divulge the information, "Savannah,"

"Ennis, I can't," she felt tears welling again and fought to reclaim her composure. "Please understand. I just can't tell you."

Anger flared his nostrils. The tears sent alarms blaring in his mind. Ennis never saw her cry and seeing it now would only reinforce his resolve. As it turned out, she was right. He leaned to her ear with a whisper, "I'm slipping a piece of paper and pen in your jacket. Wherever you're going, go the restroom and write down what's going on. When you exit the place and walk past me, you'll know what to do. Now, are we working together on this?" His question wasn't exactly a question. It possessed a ring of firmness that made the decision for her. They *were* working together whether she approved or not.

Still, Savannah debated his words. Someone still watched them. It reasoned someone would follow her into the bookstore as well. But the restroom? Doubtful. She hadn't a clue how she'd transfer a note to him without the watchdog seeing her but she assumed he had a plan. Maybe Ennis could anchor her if even momentarily. "Yes," she whispered back.

Ennis kissed her softly, "Good. I'll be waiting for you." She halfway wished he'd stop kissing her. It clouded her mind and filled her brain with thoughts she didn't have time for. Plus, he was a damn good kisser. The moment he released her she took off running toward the bookstore. Before she entered, she glanced over her shoulder. Ennis paced the sidewalk, his fists clenched as though wanting to hit someone. Though he didn't look directly at her, she knew he watched her every move.

Savannah approached the store's wooden door with trepidation. Again she found herself at what she considered the doorstep of depravity since the "Fetish Fortress" bookstore mainly carried alternative lifestyle material. She always lived by the adage "If you're too open-minded, your brain will fall out." She understood First Amendment rights but with perverts like Master Rob roaming the streets, well, Savannah's brain wasn't in jeopardy of falling out anytime soon. Thanks to him, she'd never look at a dentist the same way again...

She stepped inside the bookstore, noticing the small gathering of people around the store. Some drank coffee while they sat and read or conversed with others. They appeared rather harmless but so did poison ivy. Since their attention glued to whatever tome sat in front of them, she took a look around the establishment. She'd only seen the inside of these type businesses a few times to break up fights or question individuals about an assault. She'd never actually taken note of the inventory. Initially it reminded her of Barnes & Noble. The quiet atmosphere and soft colors with gentle music playing and the aroma of high-brow coffee lingering heavy in the air. Books were sectioned into true crime, fiction and nonfiction... When she ran across the "how to" section, her legs tried to bolt for the door without the rest of her following behind. Then, across the room, she saw half a dozen people gathered at a particular bookshelf – the one, she darkly mused, labeled "Sex". *Well, why not?*, she groaned to herself. Why wouldn't such a fine establishment carry all thirty-one flavors of debauchery?

Savannah's lip curled. Biting back the impulse to voice her disgust, she gritted her teeth and searched out the title he'd given.

"Can I help you?" The female voice came from behind her right shoulder. Despite the quiet delivery, Savannah reacted as if someone shouted in her ear. She jumped, making the inquiring redhead smile and apologize for startling her.

For some odd reason, Savannah's brain went blank. She'd been so focused that the minor interruption wiped the book's title clean from her weary mind, forcing her to refer back to the note.

The woman's smile softened when she saw the note in Savannah's hand. She reached for it, "First time in here? Don't worry, after some time, you'll know the place like the back of your hand."

She sincerely hoped not. Savannah snatched the kidnapper's note away, pocketing it. Her voice returned, albeit nervously, "Actually, I see the book right there. Thanks." She reached past the woman and as she took the book in hand, tried to discreetly hide the cover. The redhead just smiled wider and before walking off, patted Savannah's shoulder, "Hang around and you'll lose that shyness."

Savannah breathed a sigh of relief. Now to gutting through the book. She carefully swept through each page, praying the note appeared soon. The images of S & M activities began taking its toll on her stomach. Then on page 101, a single paper laid flat against the pages, the writing open for anyone to see, "From this point on, calling anyone to help is forbidden. This is our private game. Your next clue is familiar and Sacred. The Little star has how many Points? You've got 20 minutes to reach this destination. Go get 'em, Tiger."

Quickly, she pocketed the note and began her search for the bathroom and located it near a group of occupied tables. She only hoped the people were too engrossed in their conversations to observe the blushing detective slinking to the bathroom.

Once inside a stall, she removed the paper and pen. She unfolded the page and in Ennis's handwriting it read, "Our mechanic is installing a GPS on your car at Josh's request. He received a call earlier asking where to send flowers to your funeral. He panicked when he found out your cell phone was at Georgia's and sent out an APB on your car. Evidently someone hacked into the department's computers this week and downloaded your psych records. Tell us what's going on – not even Georgia will help us."

That's because she knows not to. Savannah had to commend her colleagues and boss. Josh acted quickly and Ennis prepared in case she couldn't reveal the problem – so he slipped her a note. Since their first day together, she felt she'd found her perfect partner. Sure they argued but when trouble threatened, no one was better at curbing it. She wondered if Ennis was capable of stopping this evil that suddenly encompassed her world. He was good but unless he cleverly disguised it, she hadn't noticed a big red "S" in the middle of his chest.

The corners of her mouth lifted. He might not be Superman however he'd die for the people he cared for and Savannah knew that included her. She held the note to the stall door and began writing. She explained the situation and ended it with, "Thanks for being so bossy. You're right. I need you."

5

Ennis Rutherford watched Savannah sprint down the sidewalk. In his most nonchalant manner, he took note of which store she entered. Then he nearly swallowed his tongue. The Fetish Fortress? *What the hell...* He scratched his head to divert his original reaction of falling to his knees and asking God if Savannah Prince had had a stroke. She never expressed interest in bondage or the like – on the contrary, she loathed it.

After Ennis managed to settle his rioting brain, he congratulated himself. Somehow, amid all the chaos, he'd managed to develop stone aches. Savannah was downright gorgeous and her spitfire attitude only added fuel to his physical distress. Kissing her seemed the natural thing to do. Her lips were too inviting. "You should be kissed and often, and by someone who knows how." Rhett Butler's words echoed in his mind and by God, Ennis swore he'd found Scarlett O'Hara's bona fide blood kin in Savannah. Frustrating yet irresistible.

Upon first sight of her he vowed to win her heart. Oh, he'd heard all about her through the department grapevine. The cops who weren't lining up to wine and dine her were either convinced she was a jinx to her partners or that her family's money bought her way onto the

Atlanta Police. He'd heard about her crappy luck with partners. In the back of his mind he wondered if the pairings weren't contrived by higher-ups who didn't approve of her offhand manner of police work, especially interviewing suspects. It wasn't uncommon for Savannah to smack a suspect upside the back of his head Andy Sipowicz-style or prod their memory by nudging them physically. It wouldn't surprise him if the bosses didn't pair her with renegade cops or outright criminal cops just to get her off the force. Ennis noticed, however, she only resorted to physical force when kids were victims of a crime. Savannah, like everyone with a brain socked between their ears, hated people who hurt kids. But it lit a fire under her Ennis had never seen before. It was through their boss, Josh Hunter, that he'd discovered the Prince children were raised in an abusive home.

Ennis glanced up a moment, didn't see her, so he sat down in one of the café's wrought iron chairs to wait. He hated to see her so upset, so… out of sorts. Savannah always had her head screwed on right. She reminded him of a bulldog – once she got her teeth into something, she refused to let go. She was rarely wrong in her assumptions and when she *knew* she was right, she was fearless. To see her floundering frightened him more than her driving. To see fear and doubt in her beautiful blue eyes panicked him and to see her cry downright killed him. Whatever had happened threatened to steal more than her courage, it threatened to crush her soul. Ennis made a silent promise to himself and Savannah. No matter what, he'd help her through this. He would be the partner she never had – strong, protective and most important, loyal.

He looked up again. Nothing. Then he glanced at his watch.

Funny how only a few minutes seemed to drag on forever – just ask his groin. Concentrating on un-pitching the tent in his pants only brought more images of Savannah and that pretty much doomed the effort. His mama would have taken a switch to his backside for some of the thoughts dancing through his overactive imagination. Pressing his body against the length of Savannah's, feeling her breasts against his chest, the warmth of her breath on his lips… God, he had to stop thinking about her like that, at least for the interim. She was in trouble and needed him.

When he looked up again, he saw her headed toward him, her hands fisted at her sides. He rose to block her path. She seemed apprehensive at the move. She stopped then tried to sidestep him. He blocked her again, this time bracing her by the shoulders, whispering, "Hit me."

By her reaction, he might as well have spoken in Latin. She stared at him like he'd grown a second nose. He gently shook her to re-establish her focus and said in a louder voice, "Tell me what's going on or I'll shake it out of you." Then followed it with a soft, "Hit me, for God's sake. And make it look good."

He noticed the longer they stared at each other, his intent dawned in the blue pools below him. So he shook her again, "I'm not letting you leave without me. I'm coming with you and you can't stop me."

Ennis knew he hit a nerve with the last statement. Her vision narrowed and he felt her tense. He immediately braced himself. Good thing he did too. He seemed to recall Savannah whispering something like "I hope you know what you're doing" – just before a quartet of bluebirds began circling his noggin. Her effort, more than effective, sent him plowing back into the wrought iron chair, his legs sprawled wide.

Ennis blinked once then twice. As he opened his eyes the third time, he felt warmth between his knees. It was Savannah, trying to appear furious but he detected more concern than anger. She stood between his knees looking down at him then fisted his jacket in her hands. With the same alarmed expression, she brought his face to hers, "You okay?"

"Just peachy," he answered, moving his jaw back and forth. He saw she planned to throw an air punch so he'd leaned into her swing. Not his brightest decision in retrospect. But to convince whoever obviously watched her every move, he had to make it believable. *But shit...* "You need to patent that right hook," he finished.

If Ennis were knocked loopier, he'd have claimed the following was a delightful dream. He felt her lean in, which didn't help conditions in his southern region, and then best of all, he felt the brush of her lips on his. It was a brief, tender kiss, offered with an apology and caress to his cheek. A silly grin curved his mouth as his vision locked on hers, "God, you're beautiful," he murmured.

He watched her battle a smile while her palm cradled his injured cheek, "I think I hit you too hard."

Baby, you hit me head-on the first time I saw you and I haven't been the same since. Her gentle touch sent his pulse racing and the blood to his groin with no detours in between. Through his haze of glee, Ennis saw her step back to leave and grasped her by the arms. She continued drawing back, her voice ringing with desperation, "Ennis, I have to go."

The joy of their brief tryst faded and the gravity of the situation intruded once more. He tensed his hold until his fingers locked around her wrists securely but not hard, "Let me help you. I can go with you."

"You can't," she replied, her tone growing more urgent.

He sensed her dread of whatever lay ahead. He gave her wrists a supportive squeeze, still debating which insanity to follow – going with her and pissing her off or letting her go and worrying himself into an ulcer.

"Check your jacket," she whispered. "That will tell you why."

The declaration didn't help. Knowing why might actually make things worse for him but she left him no choice. She kept tugging on her hands, the efforts becoming more frantic as seconds ticked away.

If he'd done anything harder in his entire life, he didn't remember when. Releasing her, not knowing where she was going or if she'd be safe without him. But he forced his fingers to open, his parting words whispered as well, "I'll keep track of you through the GPS on your car. Sugar, I don't know what the hell's going on but be careful."

6

Seth leaned forward in the rocker. Georgia could tell by his expression he retraced every step his family took the last few weeks. The caller indicated he'd memorized their habits and schedules and that he was privy to their inner workings as a family unit. Since arriving with his wife and son, Seth remained stone quiet. His only words were to greet Georgia and occasionally ask details about Savannah's job. Mostly he withdrew, searching for a solution.

There were nine years between Seth and Savannah so he hadn't had the opportunity to really know her – or she him. The many years he spent in the army served only to further alienate the two. Unlike Georgia, who grew close to Seth only to watch him walk out of her life, Savannah just knew Seth as her big brother. The one aspect of Seth she knew intimately was his temper. Savannah witnessed plenty of his and Georgia's arguments revolving around his leaving home when he did. If the Prince family was known for one thing, it was their fiery tempers and all three of R.J.'s kids possessed it in spades.

This night, however, Georgia and Seth sat together in thoughtful silence. The quiet reminded her of the many nights she'd spent alone, without Matthew, without a real chance to start their own family before he was called to the war. Seth's children livened the place when they visited, which lately was often, and it was just fine with her. She loved spending time with them.

Glancing at Seth, she knew he searched his memory for signs of trouble he should have seen, and berated himself for not seeing them in time.

She wasn't any better in that department. Just a week earlier, Lindsey and Dylan spent the weekend with her. They'd gone to Six Flags on Saturday then Sunday was Kid's Village and dinner at Mick's. Lindsey polished off the evening with the Oreo Cheesecake for dessert, she remembered. She remembered it so well because Dylan wore most of his serving home, requiring a late-night load of laundry. If someone was watching them during their outings, Georgia never had a clue. So she felt just as responsible for the current circumstances as Seth.

For the past several hours, she'd fumbled for words, wrung her hands until they hurt and made enough hot chocolate to choke the entire student body of her high school back in Augusta. She kept Dylan busy by reading to him, watching him draw pictures and finally just held him until he fell asleep across her lap on the old but comfortable bark colored sofa. Dylan adopted the Parker leather sofa since he was big enough to crawl onto it. Tonight, he clung to Georgia like a vine until leading her to it then securing his place by sleeping in her lap. Upon his family's arrival, she'd been the most composed and despite the panic churning inside her, she tried to show an outward calm for the boy's sake. He seemed to sense it and refused to let her out of his sight since they got there.

"Seth, I'm praying Lindsey will be okay." Georgia didn't know what else to say. She merely voiced her hopes.

Georgia knew Seth worried about everything – not only Lindsey and Savannah but Leah who took a Valium shortly after arriving and now slept in Georgia's upstairs guest room. His shoulders slumped as he shoved his hand through his hair, "I hope you're right. Savannah's got a lot to juggle by herself though."

She nodded in agreement, adding, "She's successfully worked cases by herself in the past. She's smart and thorough..." By his developing sour expression, Georgia realized she'd overstepped her bounds. Seth just had a way of letting a person know. She saw his jaw set and his teeth gnash. At that moment she realized how much he resembled their father when angry. A younger version of R.J. was not a compliment either. Blue eyes that were normally a soft shade of azure framed a handsome square face. Crowning his features was a thick crop of toffee colored hair lightly salted with gray that tapered to this collar, allowing only a hint of curl to appear.

Slowly and articulately, Seth answered as though she were too thick to comprehend his worry, "But it's personal this time, Georgia, and that's when things go wrong and when people screw up." And just in case she missed his point, "Because their head's not in the game, their focus is lost..."

"Seth," she called, keeping her temper under control. Someone had to remain calm, it might as well be her. "She's capable, knowledgeable and cautious."

He sighed, leaned back, and to her surprise, backed off momentarily, "I know. I just can't help but worry."

"I only wish Matthew were here," she bemoaned. "Maybe he could help."

He shook his head, "All he could do is worry with us."

The doorbell rang and Georgia started to get up. Seth stopped her by pointing at his son resting across her lap, "You're sorta busy. I'll get it."

Dylan sleepily mumbled his disgruntlement at the interruption. Georgia stroked his hair, murmuring, "Go back to sleep, sweetheart. It's okay."

Seth opened the door and Georgia leaned to the side to see who it was. All she heard was a voice say, "Georgia still up?"

The eldest Prince bristled, "Who are you?"

"Someone who needs to speak with her."

Lifting his hands to his hips, Seth spanned the entire doorway. Oh yes, an R.J. clone if she ever saw one. Like their father, even his voice sank an octave when riled, "Let me see some identification."

By this time, Georgia strained to hear the visitor's words. She heard him grumble while searching for an ID then caught the frustrated inflection, "It's not like I'm the Landshark. She knows me."

The reference to the old Saturday Night Live skit cinched it. She now realized without question who stood at the door and why, "Seth, it's okay. Let him in."

Seth slanted a dubious glance over his shoulder at her. He looked less than elated about the intrusion. With a look of uncertainty, he allowed the man inside.

A tall, beefy man stepped in dressed in jeans, blue t-shirt and a Dallas Cowboys jacket. Atop his head sat a blue Cowboys cap that he pushed back on his head, revealing dark unruly waves curling out the front. His palm scrubbed his jaw where the dark shadow of stubble began showing. Ennis Rutherford looked absolutely terrible, Georgia noted. With his creased brow and drawn features, he appeared sleep deprived for a week and starved like a stray dog.

So when he approached her, took her hand and kissed her cheek, it threw her a second. His action seemed almost apologetic. His following words confirmed it, "I'm so sorry this happened," his stress-weary voice offered. "I'm trying everything I know to help."

She began to plead ignorance to his statement but he stopped her, "I know the score so don't bother denying anything."

Her eyes widened and tears swelled in them, "Ennis," she started then swallowed the rest. She wanted to tell him to back off, to leave them alone and let Savannah work it out herself – the way the kidnapper wanted. But looking into Ennis's tired yet determined gaze soothed her, assured her that he wouldn't jeopardize either Savannah or Lindsey.

He gave her hand a tender squeeze, "I won't let anything happen to them."

She blinked back the tears and covered his hand with hers, "I know you won't." Georgia noticed Seth's confusion. Curiosity about why she was so chummy with this guy was etched in his features. So were other, more personal questions she refused to let past Seth's lips. It would start a furor none of them could afford right now. Seth's vision switched between the two. The longer it did, the lower his brow sank, "What's going on and who are you?"

Georgia introduced the two and Ennis thrust his hand out without hesitation, "I've heard a lot about you, Seth. Sorry about my tone a minute ago."

Seth glanced toward his sister before shaking Ennis's hand, "Same here. I just want to keep my family safe whenever I can."

Georgia heard the guilt in her brother's voice. She also noticed he hadn't let on there was a problem. Knowing Ennis as she did, he knew a lot more than Seth thought. By his expression, he also knew more than he was willing to tell *her* too.

Ennis removed his cap and Georgia realized how disheveled he was. It was no wonder, she reflected. The way he and Savannah stayed at the station, it was a miracle either of them could still stand without passing out. Seeing Ennis then remembering how tired her sister looked only added to her stress. She prayed Savannah didn't wreck or literally collapse from exhaustion. Busying herself seemed the only way Georgia could cope so she offered Ennis his choice of coffee or hot chocolate. His answer was simple. Coffee, the stronger the better. She got up long enough to pour a cup of coffee but not before assuring Dylan she'd be back. The boy's eyelids drooped but never entirely closed. He was waiting for her return.

Seth waited for his sister to leave the room but Georgia still saw him glance at his watch, "You're here awfully late in the evening, Detective. What business do you have with Georgia?"

Ennis turned to him, replying bluntly, "I'm here to help

Savannah and to get your little girl back." He took the steaming coffee mug Georgia offered, inhaled the aroma long and deep then sighed, "God bless women like you. The world needs more of you."

Unmoved by Ennis's declaration, Seth's temper simmered beneath the surface, "The man who has my daughter specifically said not to involve the police. Did Savannah call you?"

Georgia tensed. She resented his speaking of their sister in such an accusing manner, "I doubt it. Why would she compromise Lindsey's safety by contacting her partner?"

Her brother turned on his heel to face her. Georgia could tell he scarcely held his tongue. From the corner of her eye, she saw his fist clench. This time, however, if he insisted on blasting Savannah's character, she'd insist on defending it no matter how pissed he got.

His voice concealed his inner anger, "How else would he know about Lindsey? Only my family, you and Savannah knew about this."

Seeing Georgia wind up for a verbal fastball, Ennis leapt into the conversation, "That's not exactly true. Our captain received a phone call earlier that prompted him to track her down for her own safety. We also got some calls about someone driving recklessly through the city, finally got a license number and realized it was Savannah. When I found her, I essentially had to shake it out of her."

Georgia tilted his head back by the chin, "Is that what happened to your cheek? Backlash from shaking her?"

Ennis blushed, "I asked for it. Literally. When she exited the building, I grabbed her and told her to hit me."

Not only Georgia but Seth grimaced on that one. The latter

decided to rub salt in Ennis's wounded ego, "That was foolish. Savannah can hit like a city bus."

Ennis forced a smile in response, "Well, she was gonna throw an air punch and I leaned in when I shouldn't have. This is one thing I can say about her. She definitely does *not* hit like a girl."

"You need some ice for that." Georgia headed for the kitchen only for Ennis to stop her, "It's okay, really. Looks worse than it feels but I don't believe I'll do that again. We had to do something to convince the nutcase she wanted me to leave her alone."

She nodded while sitting on the couch with Dylan, "Well, that oughta do it."

Seth threw up his hands in defeat, "I'm sure he appreciated the drama. Do you realize you jeopardized my daughter's life?"

The most incredulous frown Georgia had ever seen spread across Ennis's face. She agreed wholeheartedly with him. Seth was a bully and, at times, an outright jerk when the moment struck him. Since he left home for the army, she'd never known how to get along with him for an extended time. Their behavior toward each other softened if Leah was present. Seth didn't gouge egos as badly and Georgia didn't take as much offense. But Leah was upstairs asleep and Georgia wouldn't drag her back to consciousness just to referee them. Leah had been hysterical when they arrived earlier. It had taken an act of Congress to convince her to take a sedative and go to bed.

O O O

What an asshole, Ennis wanted to say. Instead he crammed his cap into his back pocket, "Mr. Prince, our captain and I care about Savannah. We are careful with our surveillance and we intend to bring her and your girl to safety without this nutjob realizing we're involved."

Georgia waved Ennis closer, "You said Josh got a phone call. What did the person say?"

His demeanor darkened. Ennis was lousy at keeping secrets from her and they both realized it. For some reason, though, he insisted on trying. Shoving his hands in his pockets, he bit his bottom lip. Georgia couldn't torture it out of him if she tried. She'd know he was skirting the truth, telling her only certain things, but flat out revealing Savannah's life had been threatened and *how* – that was an entirely different story. He hadn't even divulged everything to Savannah, why would he give the queen of all worrywarts all the details? Whoever the crazy was, he managed to get Josh's full attention and that alerted Ennis this situation soared way past critical. It took another second before he confessed, "I can't tell you but he did threaten Savannah." He cut his vision to Seth, "If it's any consolation, I believe once he has her, he'll release your daughter."

Georgia seemed to feel the resentment build in him. He shot the comment at Seth like an arrow then offered her an apologetic nod.

Obviously feeling ganged up on, Seth replied, "Well, it's not a consolation, Detective Rutherford. I don't want anything to happen to either of them."

Georgia offered Ennis a seat, "Sit down and tell us what you know. I'm sure it's more than we do."

You have no idea...   He sat in the recliner across from Georgia. He noticed the young boy sprawled on the couch, his head resting in Georgia's lap and one arm stretched across her knees like a sleepy swimmer.   Dylan's eyes labored to open, then blinked heavily several times.   Ennis winked at the sleepy child who didn't bother to lift his head but hugged Georgia's knee closer.   It was obvious Dylan belonged to Seth with his dark, curling hair and lanky frame.   The kid would probably grow as tall as his father.   His charms, however, required no refining as evidenced by Georgia's cooing and stroking his hair.   He'd heard Savannah speak of her niece and nephew and knew how special they were to her.   She loved them like they were her own.

Ennis returned his attention to the adults, "Savannah helped us as much as she could.   Gave me a note explaining what's happened and that he keeps sending her to find clues.   She updated me on her next stop.   It's at the Sacred Heart tattoo parlor in Little Five Points.   This guy's certifiably confusing.   He called her 'Tiger' for some reason.   Either of you know why he might suddenly plant an odd term of endearment on her?"

Seth and Georgia looked at each other, their brows lifting while sharing a look.   "Yeah, we know," Seth answered.   "That means he knows her personally."

"How's that?"

"That's her nickname.   I've called her 'Tiger' since she was a kid.   Seemed appropriate."

Still does, Ennis thought.   Like Seth, he leaned forward, the groove in his brow now deepening while his mind drew together potential answers, "It's unlikely to be someone who's known her since childhood. Not out of the question, just unlikely. Could be someone who's heard you call her by that name lately –"

Georgia cleared her throat with a degree of unease, "She also has a tiger tattoo and if it's in reference to that, he knows her intimately."

Sproing… Ennis swore his brain stripped a few gears but *now* he was definitely awake. A tattoo? Savannah? Really… What a person can learn about others often amazed him. Thankfully, his only outward reaction was his vision widened with surprise, "Really? Where's the tattoo?"

She tossed him a cautionary glance, "The small of her back and Ennis, if you tell her I told you, I *will* hurt you."

Ennis barely heard her. He was too immersed in a delightful fantasy involving his tongue and a certain lady detective's naked body. He could almost imagine himself sliding his hands down the velvet skin of her back. He could nearly hear her purr as his fingertips tenderly circled that tattoo and followed the tiger's stripes…

"Ennis," Georgia called to refocus his attention. "You *did* hear me, right?"

"Oh yeah," he muttered, still in his daydream. Suddenly he snapped out of it, "I'll file it away as soon as this is over."

She rolled her eyes, "Don't lie to me either. Just don't tell her how you found out."

His vision shifted to the collection of framed pictures lining Georgia's heavy oak writing desk. He recognized Matthew and then Seth's family. Another, much older picture, had two adults and three kids – he assumed it to be a family portrait because the youngest girl's eyes possessed a mischievous twinkle. Definitely a young Savannah. Among those photos sat a particularly alluring picture of modern day Savannah. A tingle in his gut traveled lower as his eager sight settled on his partner. He couldn't halt the images of her performing a striptease especially for him. He'd salivated over her breasts for months now, fantasizing about touching them – hell, even merely *seeing* them. In his mind she turned, revealing the very focus of his obsession in all their naked glory. He imagined them fitting perfectly in his palms as he touched her and made her moan with delight and – he dared brag – maybe even beg for more. It was difficult to picture Savannah Prince begging for *anything* – or having to – but Ennis wanted to try.

The fantasy swirling in his brain kicked up a notch as she gradually lowered her jeans over one hip then back up, tantalizing him, entrancing him. Just as she slipped the denim down again, his fantasy abruptly ended, like smacking against a mental brick wall. Something was missing and he knew what, "What does the tiger look like?" he blurted, his voice straining like the wishful thinker in his pants. "Just the face or the whole thing, whiskers to tail?" He motioned with his hands, "And how big is it? Just yea big or does it cover her whole lower back, like from hip to hip?"

Savannah's sister sat there, her knowing expression tilting to one side. Thanks to his eagerness, Ennis overplayed his hand and Georgia realized his purpose for asking. Sure enough, when she spoke her recognition emerged loud and clear, "Is the point of asking about this tattoo to get a better image of the kidnapper's intention or a better image of Savannah's body?"

Ennis felt only enough blood reach his cheeks to embarrass him. Then he adjusted his notepad across his lap. No sense in letting Georgia see how far his daydream affected him but he had a hunch she already knew. He smiled awkwardly then returned to his questions, "She just have the one tattoo? That might come in handy later." His vision strayed back to the picture, felt his body's fierce reaction, "With the case, I mean."

A tiny smile played at Georgia's lips, "You are *so* busted."

No, but his jeans might if he kept thinking about Savannah. That's why he needed to get back to business. He relaxed when Georgia's smile spread and he shrugged, "Savannah's a gorgeous woman. Can't help but be curious. Like the saying goes, 'Curiosity killed the cat'…"

"And you're the prime suspect at the moment." Amused at his boyish antics, she shook her head, "As far as I know it's the only tattoo she has. And remember what I said about telling her."

Ennis wanted to smile but he curbed the urge. Instead, he wondered aloud, "There's got to be a connection somewhere. Why else send her to a tat parlor? Did she get the tattoo at Sacred Heart in Little Five Points? I ask because there are three Sacred Heart tat parlors. That one, one on Indian Trails, and one on West Cleveland…"

O O O

Georgia stroked Dylan's dark hair while pondering the question, "I don't know where she got it. So you think he's sending her to places she's been before?" The instant the words left her lips, she felt silly. Savannah hadn't known about Frankie Allen Park *or* Tribulation. The latter caused her to cringe. Visiting the nightclub wasn't a big deal. Heaven and Purgatory were okay with Heaven supplying a steady diet of techno music and plenty of dancing. Purgatory was the middle level of the club and was merely a game room with pool tables and video games. Hell, on the other hand, lived down to its name. The dance floor itself served as a pick-up place for fans of BDSM. And deep in the bowels of the old mill lurked a more sordid facet of that lifestyle, one that scared the bejeesus out of Georgia the one and only time she'd gone with a friend. Knowing Savannah, if she didn't throw up first, she'd brawl her way out, telling everyone they were aberrant monsters. So, no, the kidnapper wasn't sending her to places she knew about or necessarily liked.

Ennis's vision lowered to the floor and winced, "Uh, I sincerely doubt it. Unless Savannah's keeping a major lifestyle change a secret from us all."

Both Seth and Georgia looked at him questioningly. Georgia assumed he spoke of the visit to Tribulation and yes, it would be quite a lifestyle change for her little sister if she participated in BDSM. The change would be so dramatic that Georgia would seriously consider sending Savannah to a shrink.

With a sheepish look, Ennis shrugged again, "He sent her to the Fetish Fortress bookstore. That's where I caught up to her."

Georgia gasped in dismay, her fingers momentarily ceasing their movement through Dylan's hair. Seth turned to her as she whispered,

"He sent her to a fetish bookstore?"

Dylan stirred, clearly disgruntled about the pause in attention. Georgia hugged him a bit closer and tickled his ear, letting him know she understood. His head settled closer to her stomach and he sighed, contented.

Seth waited for his son to settle down before resuming the conversation, "She's not into that crap." He thought a moment then shifted his vision to his sister, "Is she?"

Disbelief flooded Georgia's expression, "*Of course not.* How could you even ask?"

Taking offense at her tone, he answered, "I didn't know about the tattoo, did I?"

Seth's defensive response inflamed her. She launched her own assault at the patronizing man she now doubted was any relation at all, "Getting a tattoo is much different than participating in that lifestyle."

"Georgia, my point is she's got secrets I don't know about and –"

"Well, you can relax," she struggled to keep her voice low and calm for Dylan's sake. "Our conservative upbringing is still intact with both Savannah and myself."

Seth glared at his sister, "That's *my daughter* he's got. And you obviously know Savannah better than I do. I don't want either of them hurt but if she's into something that could hurt Lindsey…"

A fury so fierce swept over Georgia that she forced herself to take a few deep breaths before answering. No, Seth didn't know Savannah as well as she did. Probably because he left home at eighteen. The mere insinuation that Savannah was involved in something that might hurt

Lindsey sent her temper soaring. "Savannah would die for your kids, just as I would. We both treasure them. She'll bring Lindsey back or she'll die trying, I can promise you that."

Ennis sighed, scrubbed his jaw again, "Folks, I realize this is an extremely difficult time but we need to pull together for both their sakes. Mr. Prince, I can vouch that Savannah's doing the best she can." He flipped through his notes, stopped on one page. He waited, clearly giving Seth's temper time to settle.

Ennis's reply eased the tension in Georgia's expression. She nodded to him, offering a silent "thanks" for his input. He returned the nod, "Now do either of you recall anyone interested in Savannah that she brushed off or ignored?"

Both shook their heads and Georgia added, "Not off-hand but I'll keep thinking on it."

Ennis turned to Seth, "What about acquaintances or clients that may have seen you together? Anyone ask about her?"

Seth thought a moment. "Nothing comes to mind. We've had a few men join the group at work but no one's asked about her."

He directed his next question to Georgia, "How about unsolved cases or current cases she's working on? Anyone harassing her, threatening her that you know of?"

Again, she shook her head. Ennis blew out a breath, "Well, we know Toby Jackson's not the guy. He's sitting not so comfortably behind bars. Unless he's hired someone to do his dirty work."

The mention of Toby's name soured her expression. They'd been through literal hell with him. Ennis made a good point. Despite being in prison, Toby might have employed the work of another person. She wouldn't put much past Tobias, especially if it could hurt Savannah.

"I'll check him out anyway–" The doorbell interrupted Ennis's statement. It rang once, twice then three times. Seth simmered at the visitor's impatience. One point of his finger told Georgia to remain seated. Considering his murderous expression, she gladly did.

Seth's large hand gripped the doorknob and yanked it open. Then Georgia watched his shoulders and arms tense. Whoever it was, Seth knew them and didn't like them. He pivoted to face her, "It's Pops. Do I let him in?"

Georgia's green eyes enlarged and she swallowed hard, "Daddy's here?" She hated the way her voice sounded. She reverted to a nine year-old all over again. R.J. rarely visited unless he wanted something and God only knew what he wanted now.

Her hesitancy escalated Seth's edginess, "Yes. Now do I let him in?"

She nodded without saying a word. Witnessing the exchange, Ennis stood, "I'll head out and let you visit."

"No," the sternness of her tone surprised even her. Her vision met his, her tone softened, "I'd like you to stay if you have time."

Somehow Ennis intuitively caught the underlying message and he eased back down, agreeing to stay. Georgia hoped her sister had, at some point, given Ennis a crash course on their father's behavior but doubted it. Savannah was as embarrassed over R.J.'s drunkenness as anyone. Poor Ennis was about to have an eye-opening experience. Georgia felt awful for subjecting him to their father but she felt safer knowing a cop was present. She'd attempt to minimize the verbal damage R.J. would inflict on Savannah's partner – it was simply a matter of how much, not *if* it would happen. R.J., no doubt, would insult him somehow. He did it like most people smiled at others and said hello as their first interaction.

Deep voices mingled at the front door but Seth's was the clearest and most defined with his words, "Pipe down, Pops. Leah's asleep upstairs."

A grumble answered the admonition. R.J. pushed past Seth, his tall frame and wide, burly shoulders overwhelmed the entry as did his voice, "Didn't come to see you anyway. Where's my girl?"

"Right here, Daddy," Georgia called, forcing cheerfulness to her voice.

R.J. Prince looked like a man ready to spar with the world. Even at his age, thick brown hair dominated the gray peppered throughout, making him look younger than he was. His brawny stature still held plenty of power and his ever present determined expression dared anyone to defy him – something which Georgia normally tried not to do. The instant R.J. laid eyes on her, he grinned, his arms opening wide while staggering toward her, "Come to Daddy, sweets. He wants a kiss."

Georgia didn't move. Instead, she pointed to her lap and motioned for him to be quiet. Unhappy with his initial reception, R.J. glanced down and saw Dylan curled up asleep. The smile and slurred speech returned as he started toward him, "How's that grandson of mine? Why, he's getting big for a boy his age."

"Georgia," Seth called, almost alarmed.

This particular tone she recognized and it became second nature to react. Slipping her arms beneath Dylan's knees and shoulders, she lifted the boy into her embrace. The boy looked up at her, his eyes unfocused and drowsy. Georgia dropped a kiss on his forehead and whispered, "I'm just taking you upstairs to Mama. You can finish out your nap with her."

Dylan's eyes closed as she climbed the stairs to the bedroom. Both she and Seth did the same for Savannah as a child. When their father came home drunk, they removed her from his sight as soon as possible. No one knew what might send R.J. into a tirade of swinging fists and cursing. Removing the youngest target just became second nature.

"What the hell..." R.J. mumbled then the first sign of temper emerged, his words blended together, telling Georgia he'd imbibed longer than usual. That meant his anger prowled close beneath the surface. She wasn't wrong – when he spoke again, the ire was clear in his voice, "Where the hell are you takin' him?"

Seth blocked his father's path upstairs. He crossed his arms and stood like a stone sentry at the stairway, ensuring his sister's safe passage, "Dylan needs his rest. Georgia's taking him to Leah."

When Georgia descended the stairs, she rested her hands on her brother's shoulders, "They're both resting," she assured.

"Thanks, sis," he answered but didn't move. He remained the blockade between R.J. and Georgia. She knew he sensed something wrong and she always took his lead when their father was involved. She stayed behind her brother, waiting.

R.J. harrumphed at his son, "Cuttin' your old man off from his own daughter too?"

"Settle down, Pops," Seth griped. "I just don't want you angry at Georgia for something I asked her to do. Dylan's had a rough afternoon. Hell," he sighed, "we *all* have."

The subject of kids seemed to ring a bell with their inebriated father. His vision narrowed at Georgia, "You ever gonna give me grandkids with that good-for-nothing you married?"

Seth reached back when he felt Georgia tense. Her hands trembled on his shoulders and Seth patted her leg, "Matthew is busy protecting his country. There *is* a war, in case you hadn't heard."

Their father's vision didn't break from Georgia's, "You'd think outta two girls the married one could manage to give me grandkids. Seth's the only one holding up his end of this family." R.J.'s eyes closed and a sudden smile brightened his face, "Why, with your looks, your little girl would be a spittin' image of you and your mama. What a looker she was. God love her, she was my sunshine."

For the past few years, their father grew melancholy when speaking of Charlene. He hadn't treated her as fondly during their marriage as he had since she'd passed away. It rankled Georgia when he mentioned their mother in such a warm, cuddly fashion but tried not to let it show, "I'm sorry to disappoint you, Daddy." She nudged Seth forward and he took the hint and moved aside. She gave his hand a squeeze as she passed as an unspoken thanks. She tried to calm down. Every time she saw her father, the world spun out of control for some reason. But Seth was here, she reminded herself. Usually he wasn't – and he'd reverted to his old role of Protector. The safety her brother's presence provided eased her mind.

"He'll be home soon enough," R.J. declared with confidence. "Then I expect you to get busy. At least your babies will be *half* Southern. You got good blood so it should override his Yankee ilk –"

"Daddy," she warned. Her father inevitably spoke of Matthew in an unfavorable light. It was a facet of R.J. she did not tolerate. Because Matthew wasn't born in the Deep South, her father refused to admit the marriage was worthy. R.J. always found a place to slide an insult. His favorite dig since she said "I do" was, "Yankees are a dime a dozen but pure Southern blood is priceless."

"Look, sweets," he said as though trying to sober temporarily, "Yankees come down here with the sole purpose of watering down the Southern gene pool. Doin' a damn fine job of it, judgin' from your mama's side."

Georgia stopped listening at that point and crossed her arms. Seth did his part and slanted him a warning glance. R.J. ignored it, "Don't get me wrong. I understand you got caught up in his charms and smooth talking. Normally I'd say 'If a cat has kittens in an oven –"

"You don't call 'em biscuits," she finished in sharp manner. "Well, Matthew and I aren't aiming to call them biscuits, kittens, Yankees or Rebels. We want kids but it helps if we're together to do it. And before you get all riled up on this subject, no, I didn't fall victim to an evil genius who married me for my money and to prove it, Matthew signed a prenuptial agreement. To conclude this inane conversation once and for all, his blood is as red and pure as mine so get off his back."

Seth and Ennis stood wide-eyed at her lecture. R.J. even

appeared slightly stunned through the haze of alcohol. After a moment Seth broke a smile, "You sounded a lot like Mama just then."

She took a deep breath and sighed with a sharp nod, "Well, I've had enough of this nonsense. I shouldn't be forced to defend my husband, especially against the one person who should be *supporting* my marriage." She turned to R.J., "What would you like to drink? I've got tea, coffee –"

"Scotch," he replied, still peeved. "Gonna need the whole bottle at this rate."

"I don't have scotch," she answered back, knowing he'd basically bathed in it before arriving at her house. Pickling him further only added to their stressful situation.

A momentary flash of disgust crossed his face and he headed directly to her liquor cabinet, "Brandy then. That's your drink, right? That'll do. Hell, *anything'll* do now."

She stepped in front of the cabinet, "I'm fresh out. Sorry." Georgia saw Seth wink at her. He knew it was a lie because she'd polished off a glass earlier that evening with plenty left over.

R.J. volleyed a narrow look between his children, "You two conspiring against me? Trying to kill me off? Keep this up and I'll write you both out of my will. Now gimme a damn drink!"

Seth had enough, "You've *been* drinking. You don't need another one. I won't say it again. Be quiet. My family's upstairs asleep."

Flustered, Georgia raced to switch subjects by introducing Ennis to her father. Within two seconds, she regretted doing it, especially for Ennis's sake.

R.J. leveled an accusing glare on Ennis, "You allergic to a razor? Or are you growing that brush for Savannah's sake? 'Cause she likes her boys clean shaven like her old man."

Ennis sported the look of a shell-shocked man who didn't realize he was in a battle. Georgia noticed his hand froze in the offering of a handshake then slowly wilted to his side. She shook her head and whispered an apology. Then she braced her father, "Daddy, don't you dare start on Ennis. He's the best partner Savannah's ever had." She stopped short of demanding an apology from her father. R.J.'s fist would shut her up before the words left her lips.

R.J. appraised the young man again, "Looks better than that one thing she dragged in. He was sorry as a two dollar watch and brought enough bad publicity to choke a jackass. You look half-dead, boy. Why don't you go home and sleep it off?"

Georgia glanced apologetically at Ennis. She spoke in a whisper to prevent R.J. from hearing, "Our father is highly opinionated."

R.J. shifted to Georgia, "What'd you say?" He stepped closer, his fist clenching at his side. She watched him and instinct drove her back a step until she felt Ennis slip his arm around her waist. She knew he would protect her – and since he was a police officer, she'd hoped her father might control himself but drinking always destroyed his common sense. Seth joined Ennis and moved between her and R.J., "Leave Georgia alone. This is her home and she can speak freely in it. *You* are the guest, Pops."

R.J. contemplated his situation while facing his son once more. Surprisingly he backed down with a resigned sigh, "Neither one of you was ever respectful to me. Hadn't changed, I see. Where's my baby? Where's Savannah?"

Georgia also released a long breath. Then she couldn't resist the urge to hug Seth and Ennis both. She rested her cheek against her brother's back and wrapped one arm around him, the other around Ennis. Both responded by patting her hands.

Seth answered their father, "She's at work. She's busy and can't be bothered."

Agitated, R.J. waved him off, "I didn't come here to beat around the bush with you two. I need to see her and tried her place and came here as a last resort. Believe me, I didn't *want* to come."

Seth squeezed Georgia's hand as a sign of support. Their father always found new and interesting ways to alienate his children. When they refused to abide by his commands and words, he turned vicious, saying anything to wound, anything to bring blood. "What do you want with her?" Seth asked.

"I got a phone call. Told me Savannah was in trouble and needed me."

"That's highly unlikely," Seth finished. "You're the last person she'd actually *need* or depend on if she were in trouble."

R.J. gave Georgia an accusing frown, "'Trouble' to me says one thing, 'specially when a girl needs her father. Now what's the cur's name that got her knocked up?"

The blatant, in-your-face, utterance floored Georgia, nearly as much as if R.J. declared his membership to Alcoholics Anonymous. "Knocked up?" was all she managed.

"I brought my shotgun so all I need is a name – which you're gonna give me."

The word "shotgun" set off warning bells in her brain. The last thing they needed – particularly tonight – was R.J. loose with a live weapon, shooting at all the men of Atlanta. The image prompted her lips to move, "Daddy, she's not pregnant." *She'd better not be or Daddy'll think I'm lying then my ass is grass.*

Her father sounded skeptical, "How do you know?"

Trying to hide her irritation, she crossed her arms, "Because Savannah wouldn't jeopardize her career. Being a police officer *and* pregnant doesn't exactly add up to being practical." She noticed Seth nodded in agreement and that helped.

Their father, however, wasn't so easily convinced. He set his sights on Ennis who backed up a step, "Whoa, now. Let's not jump to conclusions." His wide eyes danced between the three, begging Georgia to rescue him. It was clear R.J. meant to kill any man who "defiled" his baby.

Their father's expression darkened, his voice lowered in anger, "You're the one with her all day. What's the matter? Can't keep your hands off a pretty girl? Just too tempting for you, that it?"

"Yes sir... I mean, no sir," Ennis stammered, while stepping back again. "I mean, she's pretty, yes, but –"

"Ennis," Georgia called in a composed voice, "calm down. We know what you're trying to say."

Even as she approached, Ennis shook his head, clarifying, "Savannah and I are partners in the police sense only, not the bedroom."

Georgia linked her arm through his and led him to the kitchen, "Come with me a minute."

She saw his shoulders slump and felt his muscles relax as she patted his arm. He seemed calmer. She understood being eclipsed by such a huge man equated to mental chaos. Getting him away from R.J. was paramount. Ennis's face paled when their father rounded on him. For good measure, he continued, "Georgia, I swear I haven't done anything –"

She arched a brow, her tone deliberate, "Ennis, I know that. Daddy's just barking up the wrong tree. Whoever called him wanted him upset and when he's upset he gets stone drunk. This guy knows a lot about our family. How, I don't know but he does."

"Georgia," R.J. demanded from the other room, "what's he saying?"

"He's telling the truth, Daddy. Ennis wouldn't hurt Savannah."

Ennis's shoulders slumped and he blew out a breath, "Thank you. The last thing I want to do is argue with that man."

Their father continued to give notice, "He better not hurt my baby or I'll be on him like white on rice. Savannah's a good girl. Now I should've taken a couple of those boys to Fist City, as hateful as they were to her. Regret I didn't. Both deserve to be dangling in trees."

Georgia saw her brother's fists shake at his sides. He took a deep breath, his expression thunderous, "Pops, why don't you shut –"

"Seth, wait." Georgia turned to R.J., "What boys are you talking about?" Toby Jackson for one, she thought.

R.J. rubbed his forehead in frustration, "Oh, you remember the bums. That bastard Toby Jackson and that fella she put away for raping and killing those little girls. He had to be the meanest lookin' son of a bitch I've ever seen. Had a name like that witch queen…"

"LaVeau," Georgia exclaimed, the reference ringing a bell. She saw Ennis palm his phone and dial the station. He looked to her, asking for the name again.

"Terence LaVeau, her ex-partner," she replied and spelled the name for him. For once, their father, drunk as he was, had a valid point. Terence's harsh features held a maliciousness that merely accentuated a cold, repellent personality. Georgia remembered an iciness emanating from him when Savannah introduced them. His thin, lipless smile served only to deepen her uneasiness, especially when he referred to her as "a gorgeous broad who shouldn't sleep alone".

He was candid about his sexual libido and habits, except the ones with children. Adding to his "charm", he often called Savannah a "split-tail" partner, a term causing Savannah to most times wince and swallow back a heated reply. She also refused to explain but said it was not a compliment. She told Georgia that Terence believed women cops were better at filling coffee cups, not squad or detective cars. When the department investigated complaints on Terence, they uncovered a plethora of sexual abuses of women and children. At the height of the investigation, they discovered the bodies of two young girls and enough evidence to charge him with their murders. Savannah was called to testify against him regarding dates, locations, and numerous occasions he left his shift early or anything out of the ordinary. As Georgia saw it, Terence was anything but ordinary and regardless of how she pressed

Savannah for details, her sister never told her how Terence reacted to her testimony. Instead, she withdrew during the trial and became sullen and refused to share even a morsel of the trial, leaving Georgia to rely on newspaper reports to keep up. Maybe something did happen at the trial. Terence didn't like women cops and Savannah hated people who hurt kids so throwing them both into the same fray, God only knew what went on. Then it hit Georgia: the note from the Camaro. "Child molesters should be spayed or neutered by a veterinarian," she mumbled.

The three men's brows rose at the statement and they all turned to her. Seth spoke first, "Excuse me?"

Georgia shook her head, "It was in the kidnapper's note. Savannah says it all the time, evidently, and this guy molested kids so it makes sense it might be him – except he's still in prison."

"Correction," was Ennis's rueful interruption. He clicked off his phone, "Terence LaVeau escaped two months ago. Tell me everything you know about him. I've got Josh accessing his records with the department and the prison."

7

"Wynngate Drive, Augusta. So many memories of the place, aren't there? None you want to remember, none you want anyone to know about."

The beginning of the next note chilled her to the bone. Her muscles tightened in an old familiar way, a most unwelcome one and her stomach instantly soured. The street name brought back images she'd hoped were long buried but even as her mind spun in a tempest of past pain, Savannah forced herself to read on, "You'll drive to 510 Wynngate Drive and look inside the old red wagon. Be careful since Uncle Bryan's son Randy still lives in the house. You have two and a half hours to drive there and find the note."

Her throat closed and a tremor shuddered through her. Someone knew. Someone *knew*. Whoever hacked into the department computers made short work of the information in her psych records. The department shrink was the only human being that knew about her encounter with Uncle Bryan. Not even Georgia was privy to it.

Savannah started out on Seaboard Avenue, slowed for the turn onto Moreland then merged with the traffic on 1-20 East to Augusta.

Once past the bright lights of the city, the route home darkened with only soft moonlight and the beams of her headlights to lead the way. The road was dark, lonely and still at that hour of night but she'd driven it plenty of times before – mostly to bail her father out of the Augusta PD jail or Richmond County clink. He always relied on "his baby", as he called her, to free him. More likely he relied on her badge, she figured.

The longer she drove, the heavier sleep intruded until she found herself nodding off a couple of times. The highway seemed hypnotizing after a point, encouraging her to succumb to her exhaustion. She switched on the radio and cranked the volume. That, along with reminding herself Lindsey depended solely on her, would keep her focused. She hoped. If not, the dreadful memories of Uncle Bryan certainly would.

Growing up, she and her family lived in the upscale neighborhood on Walton Way and across town from Uncle Bryan. The once elegant home on Wynngate Drive showed signs of a raging alcoholic living there with deplorable living conditions. Beer, whiskey and bourbon stocked the cabinets instead of groceries and ancient slices of pizza resided in the refrigerator where the milk belonged.

R.J. dropped off his youngest at Bryan's. It was one of the few times she went without Georgia or Seth along. Savannah didn't like Uncle Bryan. He smelled and liked to fawn over little girls a bit too much. It wasn't unusual for her uncle to stroke her hair or draw her into his lap with his hand resting between her thighs. The feeling made her uneasy and most times she successfully climbed from his lap without incident.

Bryan, like his brother R.J., was built like a linebacker. But unlike her father, he grew his hair long and topped it off with a thick beard and mustache similar to his namesake, Confederate General Goode Bryan. Beneath all the hair, Bryan presented a decent but not handsome looking man but his personality was as vicious as a cottonmouth snake. Savannah feared her father at times but she was literally terrified of Uncle Bryan.

Turning onto the Bobby Jones Expressway, the sickness churned in her stomach. She could still smell the bourbon on Uncle Bryan's breath. Shaking her head, she recalled one large, clumsy hand grasping the back of her hair, his other trailing down her throat. *You're Daddy's angel... So pretty...* Savannah cringed at the remembrance of his words, of his touch sliding down the front of her dress...

Savannah fought as much as a six year-old could. When his hand slid further down, she pushed it away with a stern "No".

He grabbed a fistful of hair... *Quiet, girl, or I'll tell your daddy just how bad you are...*

A blaring horn brought Savannah back to reality. A massive grill framed by two blinding headlights jolted her back, her body briefly frozen with fear. The gigantic Mack truck, complete with trailer, bore down directly in front of her, horn blasting. Savannah had no time to scream. Only instinct took over. Jerking the wheel sharply to the right, she braced herself and prayed she hadn't just managed to kill herself.

The Camaro swerved then spun while she struggled to control it. The world whirled by once then twice until the car came to an abrupt stop halfway in the ravine. The only damage seemed to be to her nerves. Taking a deep breath, Savannah tried to calm herself. She'd reverted so far into that painful part of her past, she'd wandered into oncoming traffic.

Tears sprung to her eyes in an instinctive reaction not only to the near accident but the memories. The awful, awful memories. *Pretty, long hair... Sweet little Savannah...* No matter how she tried, exorcising Uncle Bryan's predatory tone from her mind proved impossible. Exorcising his touch was hopeless as it branded her flesh forever. His fingers again found themselves at the hem of her dress and again she'd not only pushed his hand away but ran for the door. She didn't care where she went as long as he never found her. Before her hand grasped the doorknob, she found herself hoisted from the floor, her flailing futile, her screams unheard.

He was angry, so angry with her, she remembered. He tossed her on the bed, his fingers snaking their way into her panties, stripping them away.

She fought against him only to receive a debilitating slap across the face in return. His hand seized her face, forcing her vision to his, his breath sour with bourbon, "If you don't do what I say, I'll tell your daddy you misbehaved and you know what R.J. does to bad kids."

Yes, she did but when the sound of a zipper cut through the silence, the noise terrified her. This wasn't right at all, her young mind shrieked. She never heard or saw her father or Seth unzip their pants in her presence. They never treated her like this. This wasn't right...

With that internal warning, she'd fought like a feral cat, clawing and scratching at anything she could reach. Anything. Her tiny fingernails striped his arms and cheeks then her flailing fists nailed his groin square-on, making him finally release her. *You little bitch… You'll pay for this…*

Savannah assumed he meant to tell her father. Since the brothers were closer than twins at times, she knew who R.J. would believe – and what he'd do to her "for making up lies". The knowledge of that itself brought a flood of tears. She'd witnessed the horrendous beatings Seth and Georgia suffered and she wanted none of it so she played her only ace, "I'm tellin' my mama on you! And I'll tell Seth and Georgia!"

Through her tears, she ran out of the house with him close behind. She stopped only briefly, throwing every ounce of anger into the finale, "Then I'm tellin' Bobby!" It was Bobby's name that stopped Uncle Bryan cold. His oldest son was sixteen, more muscular than his father and had a black, almost fanatical hatred for him. Bobby visited often enough Savannah realized how much he despised his father. Bobby treated her, Georgia and Seth like the siblings he never had. Bryan's other son Randy was the exact opposite of Bobby and spent more time in juvenile detention than out and, like his father, enjoyed drinking and indulging in the immoral when possible. Years later, the mutual dislike she and Randy shared intensified to the point she kept her distance for fear of violence. She didn't know why Randy hated her so much except they stood on opposite ends of the law.

Remembering back, she'd never forget the moment her feet touched the front porch. She'd run smack into R.J and, confused by her tears and panic, her father gathered her in his arms, "What's wrong, baby?"

She'd clung to her father, smashed as he was, but she realized he was her only salvation at the moment – if she could part the curtain of alcohol, "I want to go home, Daddy. Take me home." Despite what Savannah threatened, she never told a soul about that day – only the department shrink. She hadn't told Bobby or anyone else in her family what happened inside that house. She couldn't allow her family to find out, plus it wouldn't lessen her pain if they did know. Uncle Bryan couldn't hurt her anymore since he died eleven years after their encounter. She'd heard he'd been stabbed in a fight four blocks from his house. She thankfully hadn't seen Randy since Bryan's funeral. As awful as it sounded, she attended only to ensure Bryan was truly gone and not a threat to her anymore.

She'd been a teenager the last time she set foot inside the house on Wynngate Drive. Randy was in prison at the time and she was helping Bobby drag his father home from yet another round of all night drinking. He lugged his father inside while she gathered all the shotguns, rifles and pistols he kept.

The phone in the passenger's seat rang, jangling what nerves she managed to hold on to. The raucous electronic blaring continued until she jabbed the "On" button, "What is it?"

"Why have you stopped?" Lindsey's kidnapper sounded impatient and agitated.

Trying to settle down from the past few minutes proved impossible. Not even his question penetrated the fog of her panic, "What?"

He restated the question word for word, drawing each one out, carefully enunciating, "Why…have…you…stopped?"

Incredulity began surfacing but anger quickly sank it, "I nearly had a head-on collision with a truck." Before spouting precisely what came to mind afterward, her brain's gears stopped then clicked in a different direction. How did he know she'd stopped? Glancing in her rearview mirror, she saw no traffic behind her – a quick perusal through the windshield garnered the same results. She was alone along the stretch of highway, her only companions were shelterbelts of trees on each side and the damn ravine she'd skidded into. A brief memory of earlier flashed in her mind. "Our mechanic is installing a GPS on your car at Josh's request…" Ennis's note sparked an idea and she heaved open the Camaro's door. Starting on the front driver's side, she felt inside the wheel well. Nothing. She moved to the back wheel. Her hand bumped against something solid as it skimmed the metal hollow. Savannah removed the mystery object and angling it toward the dome light, she silently read, "GPS." She knew the police installed one, like Ennis said, but this one, upon closer inspection, looked more like a purchase from an internet spy store. *No wonder he knows if I'm on time with the clues.*

She heard her name rattle out of the receiver so she put the phone to her ear and tried to explain her delay in answering, "Look, I'm a little shaky right now. I nearly dropped the phone."

"You're wasting time. By my clock, nearly four minutes."

She got back in the car, pulled it into Reverse and slowly backed out of the ravine, "I'm going, alright?"

"Good, because you may require extra time – if your cousin

catches you there."

"What'd you do, call him with my arrival time so he can kick my ass?" She meant the question honestly. She didn't want to clash with Randy. Her training prepared her for confrontations with nutcases but it helped if her partner was present to back her up. Even with Ennis there she doubted Randy would show his good side – if he had one.

Her question was met with silence. The man waited a moment then offered his advice, "Be quick and be quiet."

"Let me talk to Lindsey."

"You think you can give orders now?"

"I want to make sure she's okay."

"You mean alive."

"Just let me talk to her. It's not like I can do anything to help her except this."

Surprisingly, he capitulated, "You have ten seconds." A moment passed when she heard the trembling voice of her precious niece, "Aunt Savannah?"

Savannah took a deep breath to calm herself, "Baby, just hold on. I'll be there, I promise. Are you okay?"

"I'm still scared," was the hushed reply.

"I know, sweetheart. I'm working as fast as I can. Has he touched you or hurt you?"

"Savannah," the male voice scolded, "you've overstayed your welcome. Certain things need to remain secret as you well know."

The steering wheel vibrated with her harsh grip. Her whole body shook with impotent rage and fear of what he'd done to the child. She was so furious she could hardly speak. Somehow she strung together a reply, knowing it sounded as uncontrolled as the fury racing inside her, "You son of a bitch, I'll pull you inside out with my bare hands if you've hurt her!"

His laughter mocked her show of anger. He obviously enjoyed goading her as evidenced by his parting answer, "Gotta find me first. Bye-bye now."

8

Late night hours weren't strangers to her but she never liked them. It was approaching midnight and Savannah had a hunch their race wasn't even close to ending. Despite the stress and seriousness of the situation, the roots of fatigue burrowed to the bone.

When she turned onto Wynngate Drive, only a blind man couldn't locate Randy Prince's residence. Savannah rethought that. Considering the property's general degenerative state, a blind man could find it, even by simply tripping over the lawn chairs and garbage littering the front lawn – if he didn't drown in the knee-high weeds first. Plus, it was the only house in need of painting for the last thirty years and the only one with a busted screen door that hung lopsided across the doorway. Savannah noted the tattered weather-beaten sofa on the porch and a sign in the yard. Her headlights swept across orange letters on a black background warning "No Trespassing".

Quickly she cut the lights for fear of alerting Randy to her presence. The living room lights burned bright through the window telling her nothing ever changed, that he was nocturnal as ever. If she could keep him inside the dilapidated house, her life would be simpler.

Somehow, though, the hair at the back of her neck bristled just enough to nettle her. In her career, she'd learned to listen to the sign. Inevitably, it signaled trouble ahead – full blown, life-threatening trouble.

Savannah saw the red wagon sitting beside the house. Grabbing her flashlight, she opened the Camaro's door, slipped out then quietly pushed the door shut.

To avoid rustling the brittle weeds in Randy's yard, she angled to the neighbor's property and used it as the pathway to the wagon. God knew she didn't want to alert anyone of her presence, especially Randy.

Crouching on one knee, she switched on the flashlight and swept the beam across the rusted innards of the old Radio Flyer Trav-ler. The wooden sides long broken or rotted away, the wagon itself showed plenty of use and abuse over the years. In the back corner she noticed a sizable rock. Underneath, she found the envelope she searched for at precisely the same time a steady pressure in her back registered. A stern male voice brought her glaringly back to the here and now, "Who the hell are you and why are you prowling my property?"

Randy. *Oh shit...* She recognized her thirty-nine year-old cousin by his unique bass voice. It rang deep like James Earl Jones and served to caution others that this was no small man. Classmates called Randolph Prince "Raging Bull" in high school, no doubt due to his razor thin temper, a Prince trait. She figured he didn't have much trouble in prison – most people backed away from Randy and the ones who didn't regretted not doing so.

Savannah didn't withdraw her reaching hand. Any movement might be misconstrued as threatening. For a moment, she debated telling

Randy who she was but realized lying would be a worse idea. Behind her, she heard the distinct sound of a shotgun being cocked. She made her decision, "Randy, don't shoot. It's me. Savannah."

He prodded the shotgun in her back, "Who?"

She cringed, knowing his temper hung precariously on the edge. Being in prison certainly hadn't fine-tuned his patience so she repeated, "Savannah Prince, your cousin."

She heard a spitting noise. A thick wad of saliva splattered next to her knee. He knew who she was – he just wanted to bully her. His incredulous tone confirmed it, "I can't tell nothin' lookin' at your ass. You got identification?"

She felt her heart shift into overdrive. The light from the porch illuminated the area enough for him to see her hand retreat from the rock. He urged the gun deeper, "Easy. Don't want to shoot you because you moved too fast."

No, that wasn't her idea of joy either. She lifted her hands and splayed her fingers as a non-threatening gesture, "I'm reaching into my jacket for identification." With two fingers she grasped the ID and slowly lifted it over her shoulder, "See, Randy? It's me."

He plucked the ID from her hand and looked it over, "Well, I'll be damned. A detective."

She began to rise until the shotgun's barrel tapped her shoulder, urging her back to the ground. "Stay put, Vanna," his deep voice rumbled with a distinct threat. "Or I'll shoot you, detective or not. It'd be more like disposin' of a rat."

Startled at his fiery declaration, Savannah started to turn. A pain at her temple reevaluated that decision as he smacked her above the ear with the gun's barrel stating, "Turn around and I will."

She cringed from the unforeseen blow – it wasn't anything serious but it smarted real good. Plus, it made her mad, "For God's sake, Randy. I didn't come here to aggravate you. I came to –"

"What? Accuse me of trying to rape you, like you did my pa?"

Bridling her fury, she tried to eliminate the anger from her voice, "First of all, I didn't accuse him of anything. Second, if you want the truth, he did try to molest me. I was a six year-old fightin' a guy your age." Another sharp smack across her head made the barrel ring slightly, not to mention her head. "Goshdammit, Randy, stop hittin' me," she griped. "I know you don't like me but come on."

"He wasn't the asshole you made him out to be. You ruined him."

God, she wished she could face him. Not having the advantage of reading his expression added up to nothing but potential death. Bitterness laced his voice, his hold on the gun hardened. She needed to diffuse this situation quick, "What are you talking about? *I never told anyone* what happened. How could I ruin him?"

He poked the barrel at her back again, "Then how'd your daddy find out, bitch?"

Stark terror filled her. Her father found out about Bryan's attempt to molest her? Her heart would have stopped beating except it shifted into overdrive and nearly stripped a gear getting there. Randy presented her a set of odds she'd not seen coming, "Randy, I don't know. I never told anyone, not even Mama."

"Pa said you threatened to tell her, Seth, Georgia and Bobby."

"I was trying to scare Uncle Bryan away from me. I swear I never told Daddy or Mama. I – I don't know how Daddy found out." Savannah realized the danger he posed now. He thought she'd betrayed his father. Randy was the ever faithful son to Bryan. Now he could exact revenge on her, whether she was guilty or not.

Randy stuffed the ID between her splayed middle and forefingers, "Why are you here anyway?"

She didn't dare move. The ID stayed where he put it, her hands still lifted at her shoulders, "I came for a note that's in the wagon. A child's life depends on it."

He lowered the gun, pushing her aside with the long barrel, "What note?" His temper unexpectedly flared again and his large hand wrapped in her hair, "Are you trying to frame me for something?"

Memories of years prior overwhelmed her. Her heart leapt in her throat and her breath caught. She tried to control her emotions to answer calmly, "No, I'm trying to save a life. I didn't even want to come here but some freak planted a note in your wagon and sent me for it. Can I please retrieve it now?"

"No," he said, letting her go, "I'll get it." He snatched the envelope from under the rock. Laying the shotgun across his arm, he began to open the note. Savannah tried to stop him but he shoved her hand away. She finally felt comfortable enough to stand. When she turned, she noticed her cousin hadn't changed much, still tall with wide, muscular shoulders and his black hair draped past his shoulders. The only addition was his thick beard to match his mustache.

Taking a tentative step back, she read along with him, "Here's a trivia test. A Scottish swordsman battles a brutal barbarian. They both long for a prize. One's name is Russell Edwin Nash. Sound familiar? If not, look along Madison Drive near Westwood. You've got 3 hours to reach your destination. Do not be late."

Randy chuckled but not a humorous way, "You have a bad habit of pissing people off, don't you?"

Savannah didn't respond. Instead, she began putting the pieces of the puzzle together – pieces that didn't fit in anywhere. She only knew the place was in Atlanta. "A Scottish swordsman?" she whispered.

Randy nudged her, "What, you don't know where to go?"

The implication set her teeth on edge and she replied, "I only know it's in Atlanta."

"The mighty detective is clueless," he roared with laughter – condescending laughter. He got a little more joy out of the fact than Savannah liked.

She scowled at him, "If you have an idea what this crackpot is saying, would you tell me please?" She wasn't sure if it was her tone or her wordage but something set Randy off at that precise moment. He grabbed a fistful of her hair in one hand, his shotgun in the other, "Then you're gonna pay me with interest. Get in the house."

The note, she loathed to say, took an immediate back seat to fear of her own health and safety. They made their way inside the ramshackle house and old memories flooded her mind again.

He yanked at her tresses, letting her know he meant business. She reached to pocket the note only to feel the gun at her neck, "Keep

your hands where I can see them. In fact, just put 'em on your head."
He watched her follow his command then mentioned, "I have a good
mind to call the Augusta police and tell them I caught you thieving from
my property."

*Considering your prison record and the shape of this place, do
you think they'd believe you?* she nearly asked. Instead, she settled for,
"I'd appreciate it if you'd just let me go."

"What's your rush? You want to know what the note means,
don't you? Sit a spell – on your knees."

Shoving the painful past aside proved impossible but she tried to
focus. Sinking to her knees, she focused on the phone across the room.
If she could only get to it… She felt him sweep her jacket aside and
retrieve her .38. He circled around front, "I'm going to tell you
something. Remember when my daddy died?"

Her vision lifted to his, "Yes."

"Remember how he died?"

"Yes, Randy." She hated to sound rushed but each second
counted for Lindsey. Rehashing the past didn't interest her either. With
Randy, as evidenced by her current situation, it always turned nasty.

He shoved her gun into his hip pocket, "Do you know who killed
him?"

"No, Randy, I don't," she answered impatiently. "I really have
to–"

"Go, I know. But this is way more important. This is family
business." He took the shotgun in hand again and leveled it between her
eyes, "You get one guess. Who would benefit from killing my daddy?"

The whole county? She refrained from saying it however. He seemed to sense the thought and smacked the barrel against her temple again. Savannah whimpered, swayed from the pain. Randy watched her then a sudden smile spread across his lips, "I don't think you know, do you?"

"I told you I didn't," she mumbled, still cringing.

"Then that will make our meeting so much more memorable. I'll tell you who killed him but I want you to admit you lied about what happened."

Exactly, she wondered, what did it take with him? She reiterated, "I never told anyone about that day but it *did* happen."

"It did not!" He reinforced his hold on the shotgun, sighted it down the barrel, "Now you're gonna tell the truth because my daddy wasn't a pervert. Consider your confession a small payback for the misery your family has dealt mine."

"What are you talking about, Randy? My family never did anything to yours."

In a fit of rage, he flung the shotgun aside to retrieve her .38 from his pocket. He aimed it where the 12-gauge left off. "You're a liar! When a person takes another's life, don't you call that murder, *Detective?*"

She nodded, realizing he teetered on losing his control. With Randy, the simple concept of control was iffy anyway. Although she failed to follow his line of thinking, she tiptoed around her movements and answers due to his temper.

Randy stepped closer, "Well, that's what your father did to mine.

He murdered him."

Somewhere in the bowels of the house, she detected a low rumbling. The sound reverberated like Randy's deep voice but fell short of sounding human. At the moment, she attempted to digest Randy's outburst and found it impossible to believe. He was pathological at best, evil to the bone at worst. R.J. was a raging drunk and a brutal father, yes, but a killer? Even his pickled brain was capable of reasoning the consequences of murdering someone, especially his own brother.

"Randy, Daddy didn't kill Uncle Bryan. He couldn't have," she phrased it so there'd be no question, "because they were brothers. Brothers don't..." her statement faded to nil when Randy neared her again, the gun shaking in his grip.

He looked her straight in the eyes, "You don't think I'd kill Bobby if I thought I'd get away with it? Brothers don't mean squat, Vanna, especially in this family."

Plagued by conflicting emotions, Savannah remained silent. The vicious bastard had a point. He'd kill Bobby in a heartbeat – and there were times when R.J. and Bryan took each other by the throats and threatened to off each other. She'd always taken the brawls as the marinated type of brotherly feuding. How the hell should she know how brothers fought? She only had the one and he left for the army when she was a kid. "Daddy didn't kill him. Randy, they were as close as twins. It doesn't make sense. How did Daddy even find out what happened if I didn't say anything?"

His voice drifted to a whisper, "I don't know. All I know is he gutted my pa and left him to die. Someone should pay and since it was your lie that started this, it's gonna be you."

The question screaming in her panicked mind finally found freedom, "How do you know my father killed him? What proof do you have?"

Her mind raced to find a way out of the sudden convoluted mess she'd plunged into now. The whole night had been hell, just varying degrees of it, and this time her life was at stake. She watched Randy cock the weapon and place a solid grip on it with both hands, "Because I saw it happen."

Uh-oh... Somehow, this night managed to keep getting worse. She swallowed hard, ensuring she kept eye contact with him, even when she saw tears gathering in his eyes. Struggling to retain his composure, he said, "My father died in my arms, his blood all over me. All because precious little Vanna told a lie." His brow sank, his focus returning, "*I watched him die.*"

"Randy –"

He moved so close she stared directly down the barrel of her gun, felt the whisper of cold metal against her forehead. Randy continued, "There was so much blood, I couldn't scrub it all off of me..."

"Randy, please. You don't want to do this."

"Don't I? Then Uncle R.J. can bury someone he loves too. Then we'll be even. So beggin' ain't gonna help."

She watched his finger tighten against the trigger and without a second thought, launched herself into him, her hand shoving his arm aside in an attempt to deflect his aim.

Surprise replaced anger at the unexpected attack. He fought to stay upright but Savannah tackled him with the efficiency of a linebacker – she hit him low and hard. Gunfire exploded as Randy impulsively pulled the trigger, his arms flailing to break his fall. He landed on his back with a solid thud, splayed out in the floor with her on top of him.

Savannah regrouped quickly but so did Randy. She bounded to her feet and shouldered the shotgun as Randy lifted the .38 again. They both stared down the barrels of guns.

He yelped, however, when she settled her size ten shoe against his crotch, "Drop the gun, Randy."

He arched and whimpered when she applied more pressure to his privates. He growled in response to the pain, "Get off my balls, bitch."

"Then drop my gun, asshole." She watched his hands tremble as she pushed again, this time enough to make his hand open and slam the weapon on the carpet. She kept a solid hold on the shotgun and pressed down once more to busy Randy while she retrieved her gun.

He doubled on the floor, holding his groin and trying to gain control of his breathing. Savannah sat the shotgun aside and grabbed her .38. She retrieved her handcuffs and locked his right wrist in a bracelet, "Give me your other hand, Randy."

"Go to hell," he spat.

Savannah shoved her foot against his hip and rolled him over hard. Randy growled in protest, "You're crushing me."

"You weren't planning on having kids anyway. Left hand now."

"*Get off!*"

The rumbling began again, sounding more like a distant thunderstorm approaching. The longer she heard it, the more it didn't sound like inclement weather – but it definitely signaled bad news.

"I'll get off of you the second you offer me your left hand," she replied, visually searching the room for the source of the noise.

"Luther!" Randy yelled, surprising her at the volume of his booming voice.

She didn't know who Luther was but after hearing a frenzied scraping noise from the direction of the kitchen, she decided her cousin wasn't alone after all. To confirm the fact, an animal the size of a small horse rounded the corner, giving her an informal introduction to Luther.

The enormous pit bull stopped upon sight of her and stared her down, hackles bristling along his back. His large face stretched into a threatening smile that made her feel like a juicy T-bone steak in the offering. Luther possessed the largest, whitest set of teeth she'd ever seen on a dog.

Savannah swallowed hard again. Without making any swift movements, she clamped the second handcuff around Randy's wrist, effectively disabling one hazard she faced. "Call him off," was her not-so-convincing command.

Luther stalked closer, his growl deepening. "Randy," she said, finally rising to her feet, "call the dog off." She held the gun to her side for protection against an attack. She wouldn't shoot unless absolutely necessary but Randy raised the stakes higher while watching her slowly retreat to the door. Two words bounded from her cousin's now smiling lips, "Luther! Kill!"

Her legs launched her through the living room just as the snarling beast blasted into a full-bore gallop toward her. Her eyes bugged at the brawny mutt headed straight at her, his teeth bared to show every inch of their deadly potential.

She uttered a phrase that Georgia always berated her for. "God's last name isn't 'dammit'," her sister always said. Savannah would save the regret for later – if she survived this hellacious mess. Currently she put her mind and energy into a quick escape. Faster legs and feet would have been swell. She'd been dog bit during her career but nothing built as sturdy as a Hereford cow and fast as a cheetah. When she glanced back, her vision filled with the image of large teeth, her hearing dominated by the loud, gutteral snarl. If the dog managed to catch her, she knew surviving an attack was unlikely – unless she shot him which she truly wanted to avoid.

Savannah's feet hit the porch, her hand gripped the doorknob and as she looked at the dog, she noticed his eyes locked on her wrist, his jaws opening to close in for the kill. Pure adrenaline forced her to lean in and swing the door closed just as Luther pounced. A loud, solid thump jarred the door, forcing her to brace against the flimsy entry to keep the animal at bay. Rather unhappy at the confrontation's outcome, Luther scratched and barked at the door with a viciousness that curdled her blood. Savannah then decided it was time to call the sheriff on her charming cousin and his satanic Toto – if she could rush to her car before the damn dog had her for supper.

She tried catching her breath but decided if she did, something *else* would happen to steal it again. She counted to three and raced as fast as her shaking legs could carry her. The sound of the Camaro's heavy door slamming shut – with her safely inside – never sounded so good.

She felt around in the dark for the kidnapper's cell phone and noticed lights in the neighboring houses shined bright now. A couple of people stuck their heads out their front doors, appraising the situation down the street. Then, like turtles, they withdrew back into their homes. Clearly the neighborhood was accustomed to the unruly, loud Randolph Prince.

Savannah had to steady her trembling fingers to call the sheriff. She dialed from memory and a male voice answered, "Richmond County Sheriff." The deep timbre threw her a moment. He sounded familiar, like a voice from her past, "Bobby?" she inquired between heaving breaths. Slowly, recognition dawned and she was sure it was her cousin, "Bobby Prince, is that you?"

The man answered with a cautious, "Yeah, who's this?"

"Savannah," she replied, grateful her lungs were settling down now. She wiped away tears that appeared upon realizing an ally was on the phone.

His voice melted into a smooth, velvet tone she recalled from long ago, "Hey, sweetheart, you sound out of breath. What's up?"

"Your brother, unfortunately."

An urgency crept into Bobby's voice, "You're at the house? Are you okay?"

"Yeah, why?"

"I'm on my way there now. We had reports of gunshots from the house. What are you doing there?"

She gave him a rundown of the previous several minutes only to have him cut her off partway into the explanation, "Wait. Are you still in the house?"

"No, not since I got an up close and personal with a mammoth named Luther."

Bobby released a sigh, "As long as you're okay. Just stay outta that house until I get there. I know how to deal with Luther."

"Good thing you do or most of Richmond County would be digested by now."

"I'm sorry about this. Randy's never been balanced but there's no excuse for what he did. I'll round him up and throw him in the pokey. And as for that mutt, he's going to the pound for the last time. Randy trained him to be just like him – mean as a damn viper."

Randy's words still stung fresh in her brain and she eked into the subject carefully, "Bobby, I need to…" her voice trailed off when a hint of doubt crept in. Randy was a Class A liar, everyone knew it. Mentioning Uncle Bryan's death to Bobby meant finding out the honest truth. Did she really want to know? "I need to ask you about Uncle Bryan."

"What about him?" the warmth in his voice vanished and she nearly regretted bringing it up. Then, as though realizing his harshness, Bobby softened again, "I mean, he did enough damage to you when he was alive so why exhume any painful memories?"

"That's just it. How do you know what happened?"

Bobby went stone silent and it seemed to take a moment to recover from the unexpected question, "Vanna, you might not have said a word but when Pa got drunk, the news traveled."

Well, this isn't sounding very hopeful… "Did," she paused to rephrase her thoughts. Pandora's Box wasn't just open, someone wedged a titanium bar inside, preventing it from ever closing so she might as well ask, "Did Daddy find out?"

She could sense him cringing as he replied, "'Fraid so. He told your ma and your sister and brother. Seth is the one who told me." He faltered as if weighing whether to speak again and Savannah waited. Eventually he continued, "Van, I'm sorry my father did what he did. He was an evil bastard but I never knew until then just how evil he was. When I heard about the panties on the bed, I wanted to kill him myself."

A flash returned of leaping from the bed, terrified out of her mind. At the time, the last thing she thought or cared about were her panties. She agreed his father was a detestable creature but Bobby turned out exactly opposite of him, "Bobby, please don't apologize for him. You didn't do it and you couldn't change Uncle Bryan like I can't change Daddy. Who found the panties?" she asked.

"Uncle R.J. did." Bobby's answer stole the breath from her. "Evidently after he put you in the car, he went back inside to confront Pa about why you were crying and the rest is pretty much history."

Oh my God. It's true. For once, Randy was right. She decided the baptism of fire, painful as it probably would be, was the right road to take. After all, she needed to know for sure and she trusted Bobby, "Who killed Uncle Bryan?"

An ominous silence overshadowed their conversation for several seconds. She heard him take a deep breath as if to answer, then heard him exhale, giving way to quiet once more. Savannah half-feared he'd confirm Randy's revelation, "Bobby?"

"Yeah, I'm still here," he replied, resigned. "It's in the past,

Vanna. *No one* saw anything and if they did, you couldn't get anyone *legitimate* to say so. Get me?"

Yes, someone saw everything and no one wanted to investigate. As if affirming her thoughts, Bobby continued in his best fatherly tone, "Everybody knew what he was, no one wanted their kid to be a victim. Randy's obviously said something to you but it's best you leave it to rest."

For the moment her life was hell anyway. Until she found Lindsey, this news had to take a back seat. Bobby wanted it dropped – See No Evil, Hear No Evil, Speak No Evil and the more she thought about it, Bobby had a splendid idea.

9

Ennis paced the kitchen floor. He'd tried to convince Georgia, Seth and their father to take a nap or rest upstairs while he monitored the situation via telephone with the forensics team. None of them took his advice. Instead, Georgia busied herself with making coffee and discussing possibilities with Ennis. Seth joined their conversation at times, others he stayed to himself clearly working through the situation in his own way. R.J. sat quietly in Matthew's recliner but still made occasional remarks about Savannah's ex-partners and ex-boyfriends.

Georgia glanced around her living room. Taking stock of the assembled group, she shook her head. What started out as a good day sure did turn to crap. When her vision met Ennis, she saw him staring at Savannah's portrait on the coffee table. Even from across the room, Georgia felt him pining for her sister. Mr. Rutherford felt more than a sense of duty toward Savannah, she'd bet her inheritance on it. She'd bet every penny of her next royalty check that Ennis was in love. They hadn't been together long – less than a year – but from day one, Georgia had a hunch he treasured the partnership in many ways. Tonight proved it without a doubt.

To her knowledge, he'd not eaten since that morning when he

and Savannah existed on Milky Ways and coffee. He said he'd only slept an hour when their captain called him back to the station about Savannah. Since arriving at Georgia's house, pacing became his new hobby – besides gravitating to any photo or portrait she had of Savannah. Occasionally he held one with a wistful stare. On the surface Ennis suffered from the evening's stress, but in her opinion, his heart was hurting the most.

Georgia watched him approach the coffee table. He'd discovered a new image to fret over. This time, she noticed, he'd chosen the portrait of Savannah in uniform. He reverently removed it from the table and began to stare again. "The Exceptional Merit Medal?" He seemed rather surprised, she noticed, as he took closer note of the breast bars on her uniform. "And four commendations," he turned to Georgia. "Do you know what it takes to receive the Exceptional Merit Medal?"

Yes, she did, because she'd seen Savannah through the aftermath. Georgia gave a slow nod, indicating she knew very well, "She saved a fellow officer from dying in the street – while under fire."

Ennis's chest broadened with pride and he smiled, "Sounds like her, all right."

"She paid for it though. The gunman shot her before she could drag the officer to safety." Georgia regarded his stunned expression and answered his unspoken question, "The arm," she tapped a spot near her shoulder. "She switched hands, pulled the officer along with her good arm and started shooting at the suspect as she went."

"Now that *does* sound like Savannah." He gazed at the picture a moment, his features turning grave, "I should have never let her go. I should have followed her no matter what she said or did."

"Ennis, you did the right thing. This guy is watching her." She waited for his vision to meet hers, "You did the only thing you could."

Movement on the stairway halted their conversation. Georgia leaned back to see Leah ambling down the stairs, her steps tentative and unsteady. Viewing her sister-in-law teeter then white knuckle the railings, Georgia charged from her chair to support Leah and guide her to the recliner next to R.J.. She fetched a cup of coffee and Leah accepted it with trembling hands and a quiet thanks. "Have you heard anything from Savannah?"

Georgia hated to answer that question. Fact was no one had heard anything since Ennis appeared at the front door. She shook her head, "Nothing yet but don't give up hope." Her heart ached for Leah. The woman's eyes were swollen and red from crying, her face pallid and drawn. Georgia could only imagine the anguish she endured, a mother worried sick – literally – about her child. Georgia placed her hand on Leah's arm to reiterate, "Please don't give up."

With a weak smile Leah nodded. Ennis's mouth opened to reinforce the message when his cell phone rang. Everyone in the room turned to him as he answered it. He stood a moment then Georgia saw his brow wrinkle, "What? How long has she been there? Wait a minute," he looked at Georgia. "You grew up in Augusta, right?"

Georgia nodded. Seth's interest wavered between his sister and Ennis, "Why does that matter?"

Ennis lifted his hand as a request for silence while he listened to the caller then, "Who lives at 510 Wynngate Drive? That your address?"

A shiver shook Georgia while memories flooded back. R.J. stomping in the house with young Savannah on his hip... Her little sister's face red and tear-streaked... R.J. setting Savannah down, the child running toward her, her arms grabbing tight around Georgia's waist... Georgia glancing back as their father retrieved a pair of small pink panties from his coat pocket... R.J. grinding the words "I'll kill him" past his clenched jaw... The gravity of the moment hit her equally as hard now as then.

The same sick feeling plagued Georgia then the guilt set in. She couldn't save Savannah then but it was different now. Someone had to save her sister from the evil in that house. Bryan was dead but Randy was a fresh hell the Prince family readily denied association with.

Georgia couldn't just sit around anymore, not after hearing that address. She angled past Ennis to her Tahoe keys hanging on the wall. Seth hustled from the dining table to meet her, "Where do you think you're going?"

"Randy's house. She's in trouble if she's there."

Having seen the panic in her eyes, his hands grasped her arms, "Georgia, it's over two hours to Augusta. You can't possibly help her."

Her voice was a mixture of anger and fear, "I have to try. Seth, you *know* what that family's capable of." Cutting her eyes, she noticed Ennis approaching and lowered her voice, "Randy's no better. He buried kittens alive and gutted a neighbor's dog and that's when he was a kid. We know what he's been in prison for – Savannah's in real danger with him. If something happens to her, I'll never forgive myself for not trying..."

Her brother brought her into his embrace, his strong arms providing solace she'd not felt in years. Georgia clung to him, again grateful for his strength and composure when hers seemed to falter so quickly. However, when a person dealt with Bryan or Randy, it wasn't prudent to assume anything, much less anything good.

Seth's voice eased from authoritative to reassuring, "I didn't call her 'Tiger' because she has stripes. The kid has spirit. She's a fighter and she'll be okay. Someone told me earlier that she was smart and capable. Well, she's also strong. Now let me have the keys."

Georgia slowly parted from the embrace and looked in her brother's eyes. Like reverting back to childhood, Seth presented a comforting air that settled her better than anyone could. He had certain manner that no one else did and she handed him her car keys.

Ennis closed in on Georgia and Seth's powwow, "Did I hear you right? This guy buried animals alive?" Shock yielded quickly to anger, "Who is he?"

"What address you say?" R.J. inquired. Without breaking eye contact with Savannah's sister, Ennis repeated it for their father.

R.J. shot from the recliner, "What the hell is she doin' there?"

His nostrils flared, Ennis looked to the brother and sister for an answer, "Georgia, I need information now. Who is this guy you're talking about?"

If Seth hadn't put his arm around her, she wasn't sure she could describe the evil residing at 510 Wynngate Drive. "That's our Uncle Bryan's house. He died several years ago but he left the house to his son Randy." She heard her voice taking on the alarm it had when she heard the address. "His name is Randolph Prince. He's got a prison record, Ennis, and it's not for theft, if you know what I mean."

Picking up on Georgia's distress, Ennis's brow sank and his jaw set. He realized how serious the situation was and he returned to his companion on the phone, "Run a Randolph Prince through the system. He owns the property now."

"Sonuvabitch house should've been burned down with Bryan in it," R.J. lashed out. The outburst brought everyone's attention to him as he stalked toward Ennis – in a strangely sober manner. "Coulda saved us all this trouble."

Ennis stepped back and Seth, recognition in his eyes, warned, "Pops, don't kill the messenger. Ennis is only trying to help."

R.J. stopped a few feet short of Ennis, demanding, "What's my baby doin' at that bastard's house?"

Ennis swallowed hard, "According to the GPS, she's been there for about thirty minutes. There's been no movement in that time."

Georgia tried freeing herself from Seth's hold but her brother reinforced it by embracing her again. She gave Seth a pleading look but he shook his head, "You're staying here, sis."

Ennis turned his attention to the voice on the phone, "Give me a rundown on this guy." As he listened, Georgia saw the color drain from Ennis's cheeks and he swallowed dryly, "I see. Tell the captain I want to coordinate with Augusta PD. We're moving in and getting her the hell out of there."

Georgia breathed a sigh of relief. Ennis was going to save Savannah. Seth hugged her close and she returned the gesture. Maybe she could begin breathing again and stop fretting and stop obsessing. Once she knew Savannah was safely away from the house – away from Randy – she could. Randy was a mean son of a bitch, she remembered. She swore he'd grow up to be a serial killer and she hadn't been short of wrong. In the past he'd maimed people for pure enjoyment, stopping just short of killing them but leaving them with devastating physical and emotional scars. To have Savannah in his hands was as unspeakable as seeing her with Ted Bundy. Bryan – the mere mention of his name turned her cold. She knew what he'd tried to do to Savannah and God forgive her, she was damn glad he was dead. The thought of sheer hatred made something click inside her brain. Something that wasn't bad for a change. While Randy was evil waiting to happen, Bryan had another son – one as good as gold, "Bobby!" She ran to the phone but before she picked it up, Ennis stopped her, "What are you doing? Who's Bobby?"

"Randy's brother Bobby is the Richmond County sheriff now. Let's get him to check the house."

Ennis's eyes tightened as he considered her statement. She precisely read his thought – if Bobby was Randy's brother, chances were he was an asshole too. Georgia tried to ease his concern, "Bobby's a good guy. Trust me, Ennis. He'll help."

Ennis finally agreed, "Call him."

Georgia dialed the number from memory which surprised her. It had been months since she'd seen Bobby. The thought depressed her too. He was basically all alone in Augusta. His brother ignored him and she was sure R.J. hadn't exactly extended a welcome mat, not unless its name was Jack Daniels.

"Richmond County Sheriff's Office," said a male businesslike tone.

"Hello, Bobby."

The voice softened, "Now this sounds amazingly like Georgia. This is the night for family reunions evidently."

She hated to get her hopes up, "What do you mean? Have you seen Savannah?"

"Yeah. In fact, she just left. I had to make a run out to the house. Randy's up to his old tricks again and I had to bring him in. What's going on up there anyway? She wouldn't tell me anything except Seth's daughter is in trouble." He hesitated then finished, "Did Randy have anything to do with it?"

Georgia breathed a sigh of relief. Seth, who'd been listening beside her, hugged her close. The news that Savannah had just left made it sound like she was okay. She shook her head, "No, Bobby. He was only involved because he knew Savannah. How did she look? Is she okay?"

"She's okay but dog-tired. I gotta hand it to the girl. Even at this time of the morning she's got spunk. She did say Randy didn't hurt her but the way I found him it's no surprise. She trussed him up something tight."

She noticed since her conversation began, R.J. and Ennis also closed in behind her, trying to listen in. "Did she say anything else?" she asked.

"No, but I could tell something's really wrong. She's always been calm. When I saw her I noticed the longer we talked the more fidgety she got. Finally just grabbed me in a hug and said she had to go. I think the late hours are gettin' her, though. She asked me about a barbarian and a Scottish swordsman that were lookin' for a prize. I told her she should really get some sleep. When she got flustered about it I told her the only thing it reminded me of was the movie 'Highlander'. It meant a lot to her that I remembered the title. Georgia, honey, make sure the girl sees the movie if it means that much to her."

Georgia knew it wasn't the movie as much as it was another clue like all the others. But to accommodate her cousin, she replied, "I will, Bobby, and thank you for taking care of her."

"Hell, sweetheart, she was taking care of business herself. All I ended up being was a mop up crew. Once I get Randy settled in the jail, I'm ready to finish my solitaire game. I hate it when he acts up but he's never been a sweet little bastard."

10

Once Georgia updated everyone on her conversation with Bobby, Ennis took time out to refill his coffee cup. He absently poured in two spoonfuls of sugar and stirred it in.

He couldn't help but notice Savannah had a very weird family – certifiable in some ways. Georgia and Savannah evidently were the only two centered ones of the bunch because so far he'd met an explosive drunk who served as her father and a brooding, selfish bully who supposedly was her brother. Seth's wife and kid seemed okay, but branches off the Prince family tree really gnarled up past that. Randy and his father were bona fide specimens of evil. Against Seth's advice, Georgia clued Ennis in on "Uncle Bryan" and his past behavior toward children. She stopped short of actually naming Savannah but Ennis wasn't stupid. He knew the cruelties adults could inflict on kids. He'd seen it first hand but to learn Savannah suffered at the hands of her uncle, well, if Ennis could have possibly killed Bryan twice, he would have.

Then there was good old Randy. When the background check returned and his colleague read the charges to him, Ennis nearly puked. Assault with intent to kill, assault on a police officer while armed, first degree sexual abuse, malicious disfigurement, and that was when Ennis felt his stomach reel. He'd stopped his colleague from reading at that point.

Randy should have racked up the mother of all prison terms but amazingly he walked free after a few years. Ennis had a feeling even the felonious side of the Prince family carried a lot of weight in Augusta. Still, when a predator roamed the streets, besides six feet under, prison was the best place for them.

Randy possessed no morals, ethics or manners in any respect. He didn't care who he hurt or how. And Savannah had been in his house against her will. According to Bobby (clearly not all the Bryan Prince genes soured before producing a decent child) Randy held her at gunpoint and sicced a giant canine on her but she'd managed to escape unscathed. For Randy's sake, Ennis hoped Bobby was right. If he saw one scratch on his partner, Ennis planned to visit Mr. Randolph Prince with his little friend Smith & Wesson.

Ennis could imagine Savannah's reaction to the mutt. While making a quick exit, she probably uttered her favorite curse, "Shee-yet," in that heavy Southern drawl. She didn't possess a thick twang until she uttered certain words – "shit" being foremost.

Demure certainly wasn't how he'd describe his partner. She stood up to anyone who opposed her and voiced her feelings in an up front, no nonsense fashion only a numbskull could misunderstand. His country raising led him to believe Southern women batted their eyelashes to sway a man's thinking and if that didn't work, they'd sway their hips. All while tempting him with their hypnotizing drawl, y'all, and charmin' them right down the aisle.

Ennis smiled a little. Savannah wasn't *anything* like that. She didn't exaggerate the alluring sway in her hips, as if she realized the natural fluid swing spellbound him beyond words. She batted her eyelashes at him when she really wanted something, yes, but it always involved police work. And that drawl... Just a touch of sweet Georgia brogue accentuated that low, sensual voice. She used "y'all" occasionally though not as often as their colleagues. She did, however, defend the use of the word. He once heard her berate a visiting cop from New Jersey who purposefully used it to irritate her. Tolerating only so much, Savannah lashed out – in a strangely charming way, explaining that "y'all" was plural, not singular. "So," she concluded, "if you're addressing the two of us you may say 'y'all'. However, if I'm addressing you alone, I shouldn't say, 'Y'all better learn how to use the word correctly before I kick y'all's ass back to Bayonne.'"

Ennis battled the compulsion to flat-out hit the cop. Being raised in Texas, he'd shoveled enough shit to recognize a playboy's line when he heard it. The Yankee detective wasn't blind, just stupid. He lusted after Savannah simply because she was beautiful. He failed to comprehend the fact she sensed his efforts for what they were. Even when he snugged up close enough his body touched hers and she'd immediately stopped what she was doing, he didn't take the hint. But when she looked directly at Ennis, *he* knew the guy toed a thin line. Standing stone still, Savannah allowed the visiting cop to brush her hair behind her ear and whisper, "Is it true what they say about Southern women?"

She hadn't broken eye contact with her partner while stating matter-of-factly, "What, that Southern women are Mack trucks disguised as powder puffs?"

Ennis nearly lunged at the bastard when he refused to back off. The brash cop stroked her hair, his hand following the line of her back – a line Ennis dreamt about every night. Savannah's vision narrowed, her only reaction to his bold move. She was waiting the guy out. Sure enough, the guy's hand cupped her bottom and squeezed, "C'mon, where's that famous Southern hospitality?"

Her entire demeanor screamed a warning when she swiveled on her toe to face him, "I dropped out of that class before it ruined me. But I have been known to hog-tie errant cops when their attitudes roam too far *south*. Like a demonstration?"

At last the cop caught her drift – and the disgust flowing off her – and backed off two steps, "I don't understand this place at all."

Savannah smiled with exquisite candor, "As we Southern girls tell the Yankee boys, 'Don't ever think you know what's going on.'"

Ennis had laughed aloud at her exaggerated accent. She'd said it much like her sister might, "Don't eveh think you know what's goin' own."

Nope, Savannah wasn't a typical Southern Belle, a fact that would overjoy his brother Dane. He'd ask if she had a sister and Ennis would have to explain yes, but she was married. Dane no doubt would ask if she was *happily* married. Georgia and Savannah weren't much alike in personality. They were both sweet, of course, but Georgia filled the Southern Belle roll where Savannah seemed more the type to burn her bra, much less hold a death grip on Southern tradition.

He wondered how she'd fit in with his family. She'd hold her own against them all, he knew that, but how would they react to such an independent, vocal female? Swallowing a long sip of coffee, Ennis tried to imagine the meeting. He wanted Savannah to meet his mother but with Mama came the brood of brothers – Cal (with his wife Bobbi and son Monty), Dane and Jake. At twenty-seven, Ennis fit between Dane and Jake, just like a big, fat Rutherford sandwich. He'd called home a couple of weeks earlier, to feel everyone out about meeting her – and to find out exactly why he'd begun having thoughts of doing such a rash thing. Meeting his family meant one thing: start picking out a silverware pattern. He didn't want to scare Savannah to death. She'd feel smothered by the marriage innuendo and she'd made it clear marriage wasn't on her radar, at least anytime soon. Ennis knew his family. They lived for weddings, he noticed that with Cal and Bobbi's nuptials. Savannah would be a victim of premature marital plans and it would send her screaming back to Atlanta.

But for months now, he'd felt – strange as it sounded – *connected* to Savannah. He wasn't entirely sure what was happening to him. Feelings surfaced that he'd never experienced before. Possessiveness. A near feral protectiveness. And damn it, not just his balls ached these days but his heart did too. He spent all his time either worrying or thinking about her or wanting to lay her. Or all three at once – that was hardest on him. When she touched him – which she did often to his delight – a tingling thrill spiraled through him. Initially he thought she'd zapped him on purpose, to focus his attention on their task. Later, and dozens of little touches here and there, he realized she was unaware of the effect she had on him. Oh, she'd graze his arm with her fingertips or link her arm in his sometimes. On rare occasion she rubbed his shoulders and back – and his body, damn it, reacted shamelessly to her touch.

Savannah presented herself as tough but when alone with him, her personality softened, her smile gentled and her laughter became free. She worked hard but knew how to be a lady – the latter no one else in the department believed but Ennis had seen it. He escorted her to her cousin's wedding and dropped his jaw when he caught a glimpse of her all made up in a flowing amethyst gown and heels the length of javelins. She groused about the heels but once he swept her onto the dance floor, she seemed to forget all about them. His partner danced fluidly and gracefully, circling the floor in his arms. Their first dance was Stevie Wonder's "For Once In My Life". Ennis would always remember the pleasure of holding her so close, their bodies moving in harmony across the dance floor, and her radiant smile beaming up at him. Probably at that point he realized she was painfully correct when she warned the Jersey cop, "Don't eveh think you know what's goin' own." Ennis never felt so confused in his life, especially by his own heart and mind.

When he called Cal to explain his feelings about her, Cal merely groaned and mumbled something about "it happening to him too." Ennis asked him what "it" was but Cal never explained. Instead, he'd handed the phone to Dane. Upon hearing Ennis's quandary, Dane laughed so hard, Ennis thought seriously about flying to Texas just to hit him. Then to rub salt in the wound, Dane, between heaving breaths, enlightened his younger brother, "Ennis, old boy, you're doomed."

"Doomed? What the hell are you talking about?"

"You're in love." The words didn't piss Ennis off. His brother's manner did and before hanging up on Dane, Ennis heard him declare, "And I sincerely pity that poor woman…"

11

The parking lot of Kurgan's restaurant and pub presented yet another challenge in the bizarre night. She circled the parking lanes three times before finding an empty slot. As with Tribulation, Kurgan's presented itself benignly enough from the outside. She dreaded going in, though. Nearly every stop except the Sacred Heart tattoo parlor and Frankie Allen Park seemed to upset, offend or threaten her in some way. After Bobby reminded her of the movie Highlander, her weary brain somehow scrounged a recollection of the characters Connor MacLeod and his enemy Kurgan.

She stepped inside and smacked into a thick curtain of cigar smoke that stung her eyes and choked her. Once she waded further in, the curtain faded slightly, allowing her eyes to adjust to the dim lighting. Dark paneled walls gave the place an ominous air but not as ominous as the two medieval axes hanging above the entrance.

Over each private booth was a long, black wall torch that provided enough light for the immediate area. Mounted above the torches were knight and Lionheart shields and double ball flails, the latter crossed in an "X".

Allowing not only her eyes but psyche time to adjust, she noted the two giant iron chandeliers looming over the section between the booths and bar. A suit of armor stood sentry at the door – holding menus – while waitresses dressed in black leather and high heels traipsed about, delivering food and drink. So much for a *true* medieval experience. If those particular waitresses ever served the male masses way back when, Savannah figured war would be the last thing on their minds.

The ambiance of the place was a bit overwhelming at first then it became downright intimidating when she took note of the women patrons. *Great. I'm in a biker bar*, she bemoaned to herself. Tattoos covered most of the female skin in attendance – skulls, crossbones, gargoyles and the like – and it gave her, as her mother so eloquently put it, the heebies. Generally it wouldn't but when every head in the place swiveled to her and a hush fell over half the establishment, a few butterflies took flight in her gut. *One of these things is not like the others*, the song went. *One of these things just doesn't belong...* It didn't take a genius to figure out which one it was, either. She was grateful to have her jacket on for two reasons. One, to hide the badge on her belt and two, for hiding her *un*-tattooed arms from the masses. She already felt out of place, no need to show how much out of place she really was.

Savannah perused the patrons, unsure of how to obtain her next clue. Surely the kidnapper had a way of getting the clue to her. Maybe he just wanted her to wait. No doubt he wanted her to worry.

Her heart pounded and her face flushed from dashing from place to place with scant time available to lose. She took a moment to stand

and catch her breath – a precious commodity since the whole disaster began. The pervert had her running all over Atlanta – correction, *the state of Georgia* – for clues that never revealed a shred of help concerning Lindsey but merely plunged her further into his convoluted plan – and reinforced her exhaustion.

After a bit, she angled toward the bar and sat down. He'd given her approximately thirty minutes for this leg of the journey. "Coffee, please," she ordered. "And if it's strong enough to run the Boston Marathon, I'll take two."

After an appraising glance at her new customer, the female bartender went to work. Savannah took the time to survey the people in the place again. People ate their meals in private booths while the singles took to the counter or bar with their meals. The waitress sat a large stein in front of her causing Savannah to stare incredulously at the size. She hadn't known she'd ordered a half gallon of coffee. But hey, she ultimately relented, she needed the boost.

"What can I get you to eat, Detective?" the girl inquired.

The coffee took a back seat upon being addressed by her title. Déjà vu smacked her squarely in the fatigued lump she lately referred to as a brain. The last time a person addressed her by her title, he resembled someone out of Mad Max.

She looked up, guarded, at the waitress who pointed to Savannah's belt, offering, "Gold shield. My grandpa had one too."

Releasing a long, somewhat steady breath, she shook her head, "No time for food, plus my appetite isn't there but thanks." She slid a ten dollar bill across to the waitress, "Keep the change."

The girl's eyes lit up, "Thank *you*, Detective. If you need anything, just let me know."

"This may sound strange but you wouldn't happen to have a note or envelope for me, would you?"

The girl's features drew into a confused frown, "No, were you supposed to meet someone here?"

Savannah managed a weak smile, "I wish I knew. Thanks anyway." She lifted the stein to her lips and noticed her hand shaking. It had been a long, exhausting night and it wasn't near over yet. Steadying the stein with both hands, she blew the steam off and indulged in a tentative sip. The coffee tasted strong enough to take over small countries but it refreshed her, gave her time to think. She'd take the time to work on who the kidnapper was. Fatigue set in heavily on her brain, making it churn as though slogging through a giant mud hole. While drinking her coffee, she reviewed old boyfriends, acquaintances, and cases. The waitress topped off the stein while Savannah checked off potential suspects.

A touch on her shoulder made her tense and wheel on the barstool. She found herself face to face with Seth, his face drawn from stress. "Hey," he greeted tiredly and hugged her.

As fast as her adrenaline surged, it ebbed even faster upon seeing her oldest sibling. She wrapped her arms around him, "Hey, big brother." Considering the present clientele, Savannah figured they resembled Greg and Marcia Brady crashing an Ozzy Osbourne bash. People still stared at them, sizing them up, curious why they encroached into their domain.

Seth folded his large frame onto the neighboring barstool, giving the group a fleeting inspection, "Sweet place – if you're Queen Isabella."

"Only she's not in charge of this Inquisition and I'm merely one of the rabble of victims. What brings you to my cozy little corner of Hell?"

"He sent me. Wanted me to give you this." He held out a sealed envelope.

"Great. More fan mail."

"He had it under Georgia's welcome mat. He called and told me to deliver it within 20 minutes. I drove 80 to get here in time."

"Welcome to my world," she mumbled and wearily plucked the note from his hand. She began to open it but Seth stopped her with a hand on her wrist, "He said wait ten minutes to open it. Why, I don't know." He waved off the approaching waitress to assure their privacy.

"Who does with this asshole? This guy has me going everywhere. It's like trying to herd cats. You can't keep up."

"Pops thinks he knows who it might be. First, how are you after scrapping with Randy? Did he hurt you?"

Savannah sensed the intent of the question, especially when he visually checked her over then settled on her eyes. He was searching for obvious hesitation or answers she might withhold. She smiled a bit. Seth still wanted to protect her. Then she shook her head, "No, I handled it with Bobby's help."

Seth patted her hand, "Good. Bobby's always been a good guy. Now, Pops thinks this freak is your old partner Terence LaVeau. Ennis checked it out and he escaped two months ago. No one notified you of it?"

Savannah descended into dark memories of her ex-partner, absently replying, "I don't check my mail that often. Guess this'll teach me – if I live through it."

The news both came as a revelation and a condemnation. Either way, she could begin to possibly put a face with the bastard. Her father put the words to Terence's appearance as "fell out of the ugly tree and hit every branch on the way down." Even at the time Savannah thought it was appropriate. Learning the kidnapper's identity should have affected her more, but she'd spent so much time playing his game to save her dear niece, he could have been Santa Claus and she'd kill him without one guilty pang in her soul. Protecting herself adequately while trying to save Lindsey, however, would be impossible. Terence was ex-army and had the potential to be violent when it served him.

Terence LaVeau, she estimated, had to be about forty-three now. In his army career, Terence was a Cannon crewmember. He was accustomed to long nights with no sleep and no food. Battle strategy and weapons tactics were second nature. He knew about weapons, ammunition, and locating targets of all kinds – then shooting them. The thought *she* was now his target didn't exactly produce a warm and fuzzy feeling.

"You okay?" Seth whispered after seeing her shiver.

"Sure. I'm just dealing with a psycho with army training who promised to kill me some day, no problem."

Her brother's brow sank, "Promised to kill you? And you never told me or Georgia?"

"Uh, no. Didn't seem like appropriate dinner conversation."

"God sakes, Savannah," was the terse reply. "Death threats aren't something you ignore. What the hell were you thinking?" Evidently he read her expression and decided to stop preaching. He changed the subject instead, "You said he was ex-army. What MOS?"

She took another sip from the enormous mug. It might've tasted a shade past chicory and two steps away from Pennzoil but she suspected the concoction would do the trick. "Cannon crewmember," she replied. Savannah hesitantly glanced at him just in time to see him wince. She agreed, "Yeah, I know. Of all the crazies that hate me, it had to be one with specialized military training."

"Ennis is helping as much as possible. You know, he reminds me of you – hickory-headed with a lot of grit."

Savannah swore she blushed. Just the mention of Ennis made her smile – a scarce commodity for her regarding a partner, "He's loyal and protective. I think I've finally found the right partner." The words sounded and felt right. Ennis, though a few years younger than her, treated her like a china doll. He loathed anyone who spoke gruffly to her and made it his goal to enforce chivalry to those who lacked it. Chivalry was Ennis's middle name. It tickled her that he opened doors for her, and amused her when he called her "ma'am." But the best aspect of Ennis she liked was his touch – well, until the kiss earlier that evening. After that *both* found a place in her private hall of fame. It flat out thrilled her when he touched her. Sometimes his fingers brushed along her spine when they walked a scene together. At first she thought he was gently guiding her around evidence. Then he'd done the same thing at the station which raised a flag with her along with her heart rate. *Whew...* She wouldn't even allow herself to revisit the kiss – rather, *kisses* – they shared earlier on. That was a special moment she'd take her sweet time on later...

Seth leaned forward with a devious slant to his brow, "You've finally found the right partner, huh? Just for the job or for more?"

"Seth Prince," she scolded good-naturedly, "I'm not husband-hunting now and won't be for a long time."

"Something tells me it wouldn't take much encouragement with this guy. He worries over you like a mother hen."

She bobbed her brow, "What can I say? He's just attracted to my sweet nature." Still, the image of Ennis "worrying over her" warmed her heart. If Seth noticed, Ennis must have been fairly blatant about it. Unless it concerned high-powered weapons or his self-defense studio, her brother didn't notice much. Leah practically had to bludgeon him with her feelings before he admitted he loved her too. Savannah wasn't sure he *knew* he was in love until Leah professed her sentiments first.

Seth smiled a bit, "Well, he's acting as goofy as I was before Leah took me aside and asked me if I was gay or just stupid. I'm pretty sure Ennis knows exactly what he's feeling for you so you might entertain the thought of a permanent situation –"

"After this is over, I'll entertain that along with about four days sleep." She checked her watch, noted the ten minutes had passed and tore into the note. Her brother leaned closer to read with her.

"Lucky Lindsey. She stays alive for now but don't get your hopes up. There's still lots of our adventure you've yet to experience. This clue is in two parts. I designated your brother to deliver them in person. From the time you read this note, ask for the second part ten minutes later. Do NOT open it in front of your brother. Go to your car, open it and follow the instructions. As Shakespeare wrote, 'Cowards die many times before their deaths,' and you are about to enter your private hell. Small places and tiny spaces drive Savannah crazy..." Her breath caught and she bit her lip until it throbbed like her pulse. A muted groan emerged from deep inside. If she didn't die of a damn heart attack first, she'd positively mutilate Terence for putting her, and most especially Lindsey, through this.

Sensing her panic, Seth put his arm around her, "Calm down. We'll get you through this."

"We?" The question basically squeaked out. "Can you and Georgia fit in my pocket?"

"Hey," his other hand cupped her cheek and urged her to face him. "Why do you think I named you 'Tiger'?"

"Because I didn't whistle like a clew bird?" She noticed her brother's frown lines trenched deeper. The off-beat reference to the fictitious heron that buried its head in the sand and whistled through its bottom failed to amuse him. To diffuse her crass comment *and* to see the line of his lips relax and return to normal, she finished, "Sorry."

Seth finally spoke, "I called you 'Tiger' because you don't let anything scare you from doing what's required. You have determination and a hell of a lot of guts."

His statement created a momentary smile, "What, and Georgia doesn't?"

"Yes, she does. But you express yours differently. Your nature is to throw your claws out, bare your teeth and jump in the fray. She's more of a mother lion. She's composed as a clam until her baby's threatened then the attacker better head for cover. You are her baby and I've had to do some serious talking with her to calm her down."

Savannah knew what that probably meant. A look of tired sadness passed over her features, "You've been fighting again, haven't you?"

He shrugged, resigned, "Situations like this bring out tempers but we're okay."

"She loves you. She's still trying to deal with you leaving home when you did. I suppose I just accepted it. Plus, I had her looking after me so I wasn't feeling as abandoned."

Seth's vision fell from hers, "I did let you both down in that respect. I should have forewarned you what my plans were. Just never occurred to me you'd miss me that much." He looked at her again as he gave her hand a reassuring squeeze, "I won't let either of you down again. I promise we will get you through this somehow."

Savannah gave him a wary frown. Seth returned it with a good-natured nudge, "Georgia and I might fight like cats and dogs but when we join forces, God help the bastard pissing us off. With the three of us together, he stands no chance at all. When one of us is in trouble, the other two combine forces to help them." He waited a beat then seemed to hesitantly forge on, "Sort of like the spell when Mama got sick."

Savannah bristled, "You are *not* bringing that up, are you? Not now." It wasn't exactly the time to bring up the most painful part of her past.

He backtracked to smooth her ruffled feathers, "It was an example. You're not as wild as you were then –"

Her mood darkened, "You mean screwed up, not wild. You know, I never denied it." Scanning around her for anyone eavesdropping, her vision settled on a mug of beer down the bar a ways. It looked much too inviting at the moment.

Unfortunately, when Charlene got sick, Savannah resorted to alcohol to limp along and cope with the fact her mother was dying. After a point, the alcohol became a habit instead of a coping mechanism. She found herself secreting Jack Daniels away in her house, in her car and in her locker at work. When Georgia and Bobby found out, they lectured her until her ears threatened to bleed. At times when situations grew tenuous or stressful, the temptation to drink returned. It reminded her of the smooth taste, the warmth in her stomach, and most importantly, the escape...

Most times she successfully pushed the voice away, probably because of the blistering lectures her sister and Bobby hammered her with. They put old-fashioned Baptist ministers to shame with their hellfire and brimstone. When Seth found out about her drinking, he simply chose to rage at her which he later discovered only awakened her temper and at the peak of their argument, Georgia and Bobby had to physically separate them. According to Seth's tone, he was winding up for another round and Savannah refused to have a public fight.

Tonight, she turned her back to the enticing beer down the way because she focused on Lindsey, not the bully sitting next to her.

Keeping her senses sharp was key in bringing Lindsey home and if forced to, she'd block Seth's numbskull blabbing from conscious thought. Savannah warned, "Don't further this conversation. I can only cope with so much and Lindsey is paramount right now."

Seth leveled an authoritative glare on her, "Why do you think I'm talking about anger? If you're not careful, you or Lindsey – or both of you – could die. I want you to be safe and I want my daughter back alive."

If she hadn't surpassed dead tired yet, she'd have broken down in tears. Instead, she waved the waitress down and swallowed back the hurt. She pointed to the mug down the way, "One of those, please, and hurry," was all she managed without her voice betraying her emotion. She would bring Lindsey back alive if it was humanly possible. Didn't he know that? Didn't he trust her? In her mind, she knew the answers but her body, hell, *everything* was so drained she couldn't think right.

Seth countered, "Oh no, you don't. You're not reverting back to your old ways. Not if I'm around."

"Well, I need something to drown you out and if I can't drink, I'll have to beat you with this stein."

He cancelled the order then took his sister's hand, "Savannah, listen to me. I want you both back safe and sound. When you face this bastard, keep your wits about you. That means controlling your anger. When you were a rookie cop, you let Mama's passing consume you. You were out of control, you were drinking, and at best you'd have been kicked off the police force, at worst..." his tone lowered and softened, "Georgia and I were scared if you didn't bridle it, you'd be the next one we buried —"

"Is this supposed to be a pep talk?" She gave the question enough time to hit him then, "Because if it is, it sucks." If her brother continued to pick at old wounds, she'd get the next note from him and leave. She'd had enough lectures for one lifetime, especially from a man who didn't seem as broken up about their mother's passing as she and Georgia were. It figured Terence would send Seth instead of Georgia to deliver the notes. He knew she and her sister shared a close bond whereas hers and Seth's wasn't as solid. Tuning him back in, she heard him continuing, "… trying to help. You tend to charge into situations, regardless of the danger. You were lucky back then."

"I refuse," she crushed the words through gnashed teeth, "to talk about that time. I admit to making mistakes but my intentions were good."

Seth released a long breath and dragged his fingers through his hair. He glanced at her, obviously entertaining a response then looked away. Shaking his head, he said, "Georgia said you wouldn't listen to my advice."

"*Preaching*, Seth. I don't listen to preaching. I'm reasonably sure she mentioned that word. Right now, even advice sounds like preaching. It's been days since I've had a full night's sleep and I've had one decent meal in forty-eight hours." The stone expression she battered him with was heavy enough to give him a concussion, "If I'm cranky, it's that plus the fact someone kidnapped my niece and I'm fighting fire to save her."

Seth sat, appraising his sister. Without a word she held out her hand for the next note which he handed over with a sigh. She stepped off the barstool and reminded him, "Now I'm gonna go get Lindsey." She took two strides then turned with a tiny smile, "Thanks for not calling me a clew bird. I like 'Tiger' much better."

12

Georgia always said, "Seth has a way of letting you know." Know what, exactly, Savannah never understood until now. His impromptu lecture regarding her behavior when their mother passed away told her enough. She'd like to believe it was his way of protecting her. She realized he *was* but he was also warning her not to screw up, that Lindsey depended on her to keep a cool head – as if she didn't know it already. Seth has a way... *No friggin' shit,* she thought to herself.

The months following her mother's passing were the hardest in her life. Instead of miring down in tears and depression like Georgia, Savannah decided to make a difference in her job. Her goal was to put away twice as many criminals as the best cop in Atlanta. She'd show her father and brother. Neither approved of her joining the police academy and both, she figured, prayed she'd fail and be cut loose to go home, get married and have a billion kids. Savannah wasn't about to let that happen.

She'd passed every test, scored highest in her class on the shooting range, and graduated in the top third, much to their chagrin and she did it all completely sober. Seth and Georgia, already aware of her drinking, suspected she drank on duty which she denied. Whether they believed her, she didn't actually care because it was the truth. She saved those indulgences for after her shift. Even when she was shot she was stone cold sober, but she'd have paid a hundred bucks for a swallow of whiskey to dull the pain. Sober, she later reflected, wasn't the best way to endure getting ventilated with a .45 slug.

Riley warned her it would happen. Riley Murphy, her partner at the time predicted it sure as the sun rose in the East. Lying in the warm, spreading pool of blood, she half expected him to remind her of it. Instead, he kneeled beside her, his ruddy complexion frowning as they waited for the ambulance to arrive.

Riley was a good man and at thirty-two, a damn good cop, even if he did push the department limits on weight. He could still chase down the fastest criminal out there. He just couldn't teach her to stop, look and listen before reacting in certain situations. Bulling into danger normally backfired, he explained in his not-so-gentle fashion. It didn't make the cop a hero, it just made him (or her) a dead cop.

She didn't regard herself as reckless, just motivated. When Riley held back on a chase, she bailed in full bore to catch the suspect. If he considered the situation too dangerous and told her to stay put, she took a quick analysis of it herself and sometimes jumped into the fray. After one particularly exhausting chase that had them dodging bullets, Riley braced her, "I'm getting tired of wiping your ass, Prince. You disobeyed a direct order and now, because I give a shit and followed you, we're both gonna answer to the boss." His gravelly voice forced the words between heaving breaths, "Some day I'm turning in my nanny badge and lettin' some other poor bastard change your Huggies."

That "poor bastard" turned out to be Terence LaVeau. What an ordeal he'd been. Savannah was still in uniform when they partnered her with Terence. Before they were paired, she'd heard his references to women on the job – not that he tried to hide them and indeed, the joy of riding along with him equated to having her toes pried off with pliers. She didn't exactly feel the love when they encountered danger either. If she got hurt in the process, well, that was just the job, he said. Savannah finally got fed up with him since she couldn't trust him to watch her back.

Savannah approached her lieutenant, an easygoing, good-looking man in his late twenties named Josh Hunter, to ask for reassignment. Hunter apologetically explained that *no one* wanted to partner with LaVeau and since she was the youngest officer short of a rookie, she drew the lucky number. From that moment she decided lotteries weren't her strong suit. Hunter promised to discuss a change with his captain, whether assigning her a new partner or getting rid of Terence, the latter being his preference.

In the meantime, she coped with Terence's sexual innuendo and remarks about gender. She rode day after day keeping Lieutenant Hunter's promise as her only glimmer of hope.

It was when a detective visited her at home that her concern began. He'd spent an hour with her asking invasive questions about her own personal activities and comings and goings that she grew nervous. Why were they investigating *her?* She answered the detective honestly, giving what information she could, he left and she assumed – and hoped

– that was all. But wherever she went, she felt the presence of someone following her. Whether she shopped for groceries, visited Georgia, went to the gym or drove to Augusta, she sensed the extra presence. Internal Affairs worked that way, her gut warned. In the shadows so the officer never saw the ball bat coming to knock 'em out. But she'd done nothing wrong or questionable. She'd just been partnered with an asshole and for that, she certainly wasn't to blame.

A few weeks later the same detective visited again, this time asking questions about Terence. Being naturally uncomfortable speaking of her partner, the detective decided to lay out the cold hard facts. Talk or Internal Affairs would include her in any findings they may discover. At the time, IA scared the living hell out of her. She was a new officer less than two years on the job and she'd heard the horror stories from veteran cops.

"Just keep a log on his activities as best you can. Cooperate with my investigation and I'll make sure you stay out of IA's line of sight," the detective assured.

Reluctantly she followed his orders, knowing if Terence or any other cop found out, she'd be scorned and rejected by the whole department.

On one particularly hot day, Terence surprised her by radioing their unit out of service. His only explanation to his partner consisted of, "I'm tired and need a break."

She certainly agreed with that. Stopping for a nice cold Coke sounded heavenly. When they passed a convenience store, she assumed they'd pull in for a refreshment but Terence kept driving. Voicing her displeasure, she said, "I thought we were taking a break."

"We are. We're going to my farm. It won't take long."

They pulled off the main thoroughfare onto a two lane road leading out of town. They drove for twenty-five minutes past the Atlanta city limits. Savannah knew better than to question his decision about taking undocumented personal time. He'd just tell her to shut up and mind her own business. What he didn't seem to care about – what he did *was* her business because they were partners. Common sense told her that plus the visiting detective made damn sure to pound it into her brain while campaigning for her cooperation.

Terence made another turn onto a dirt road flanked on each side by groves of overgrown trees that at times scraped the cruiser's side as it drove along the pathway. Her claustrophobia kicked in but being hot and tired, she welcomed the cooler shade. Passing between the trees, she noticed the foliage lazily moving in the negligible breeze like the leaves suffered heat exhaustion like most of Atlanta had lately.

At another junction, he slowed, made a left and drove until they came to a secluded single level home with an old red jeep parked in front. Savannah recognized it as Terence's since he sometimes drove it to work.

Wild grass flanked both sides of the modest house. He'd used the term "farm" loosely, she thought at the time. Most farms actually attempted some form of agriculture. His property specialized in crabgrass.

Terence slowed for a turn and in the distance, Savannah saw a small area of recently tilled soil. Perhaps he was starting small with this "farm". He pulled into the gravel driveway with one order, "Stay in the car and monitor the radio."

He'd run off into the house and Savannah immediately removed herself from the sauna they called a patrol unit and checked her watch. Four in the afternoon, the hottest part of the day.

The oppressive heat sank to her bones causing a fine sheen of perspiration to rise along her body. The bright summer sun beat down hard on her neck and shoulders, turning the dark uniform into a veritable oven. Savannah wiped the back of her neck, at least thankful her hair was in a ponytail. It wouldn't save her from sunburn but maybe it would delay heat stroke.

The longer she stood outside, the more she longed for a cold drink of water. Since Terence refused to stop along the way for refreshments, he could damn well provide her with a glass of water.

She wandered to the front door but before knocking, she heard what sounded like furniture being moved. *Now that's crazy*, she thought. *Taking time off to move a sofa while I'm out here sweltering.* She rapped on the door, "Terence, gimme a glass of water."

A muffled response came from within, "Get lost. I'll be out when I'm out."

Giving the door a disparaging glare, she gritted her teeth, ready to unload her pent up anger. That was until she heard the cry of a child inside the house. The short yelp denoted pain. Terence had no kids, no nieces or nephews. The cry spurred her to bang on the door, "Damn it, I'm dying out here. I want some water." If she showed no signs of hearing the scream, maybe he would open the door. Then she'd visually snoop while she could.

The door came open to reveal her partner, his flushed face shining with sweat, his duty belt removed and pants unzipped. He wiped a hand down his face, "Get back in the car, Prince."

The sour smell of urine and excrement mixed with the afternoon heat and humidity struck her like she rammed a brick wall. The stench reminded her of a kennel and to her knowledge, Terence owned no dogs.

He attempted to block the doorway but behind his shoulder Savannah spied little Rachel Ballard naked and crying in the living room. In those brief moments, the female cop remembered the girl's photo on TV and the flyers handed out to law enforcement. They even carried one in their car and that very morning she'd wondered aloud about Rachel's whereabouts. In his usual diplomatic way, Terence answered, "Wherever she is, she's dead. Guaranteed."

Rachel had been missing two weeks and here she stood, gagged with her hands bound to a railing separating the kitchen and den. She looked nothing like the school picture her parents provided police. Her once silky brown hair now fell in tangled strings around her shoulders and her tear streaked face showed signs of constant crying. Bruises from Terence's fingertips spotted her shoulders, arms and thighs.

Savannah felt the air leave her lungs as disbelief ruled her brain. *A cop* had the girl all along. Not just a cop but *her partner.* Savannah's vision lowered to Terence's crotch as he zipped his uniform slacks. His head slowly turned to appraise the scene behind him then his cool, even stare returned to Savannah, "Prince, I want you to listen close to what I'm about to say."

She didn't like his expression. It telegraphed his rage without him saying a word. She met his unblinking gaze as he continued in a low, calm tone, "I know where your sister lives and she's all alone in that big house. For her sake, I strongly advise you to forget everything you *think* you've seen here..."

And that's when Savannah decided to take action. The Thin Blue Line didn't apply to child molesters or cops who threatened another officer's family. She slipped her gun from its holster, leveled it in one hand and ordered him to step aside. He had. Savannah stepped closer to Rachel as the girl's eyes pleaded for help.

Terence chuckled as if his partner's stand was a joke, "She's not going anywhere." His brow sank toward Hell, "March your ass out to the cruiser now."

"Not unless Rachel comes with me." Savannah reinforced her stance, her left hand lifting to steady the heavy gun.

Terence stalked closer, disregarded the weapon pointed at him. Before she was able to steady the weapon, Terence gripped the barrel to remove it from her possession. Savannah saw her one and only chance and pulled the trigger as the aim veered in his direction.

Terence jerked, his features flinched. The curse he uttered and the trail of blood trickling down his arm informed her she'd hit her mark somewhere close to his shoulder. Amazingly impervious to the pain, Terence's grasp on the gun hardened, "You wanna kill me?"

"Yes," she answered, trying to retain custody of her weapon and gradually losing the battle.

Through clenched teeth Terence asked, "You want me dead, don't you, Prince?"

"Yes!" Even with both hands locked on the gun, her partner gained control.

Terence twisted the gun and her arm behind her.

Savannah whimpered as he pushed her arm past its limit, forcing her to release the gun. Using his strength and weight, Terence shoved her out the door.

She stumbled but managed to retain her footing. Turning, she faced the barrel of her own gun. Terence's mouth curled into a malicious smile, "Then turnabout's fair play, dontcha think?"

With the gun still pointed at her, Savannah turned and ran toward the cruiser just as he fired a shot. Another shot rang out as she ducked behind the car. Bullets plinked off the hood and side of the cruiser as Terence emptied her duty weapon. If he'd aimed at her, she'd have been long dead. Unless he meant to scare her to death – or, she feared, he was reloading...

Savannah opened the cruiser door, leaned inside and called for backup. She replaced the mike back on the radio and eased back out of the car – until she bumped into something.

Swallowing hard, she turned, seeing her partner standing over her, her gun still in his hand. "Bitch," was all he said as he lifted the gun. Savannah tried to duck the blow but Terence belted her with the butt of her weapon and a black curtain swept across her consciousness.

She wasn't sure how long she was out but once she awakened, police officers swarmed around her and the property. The red jeep was gone. Voices mentioned Terence's name. Others announced they'd found him driving north on I-75. Thankfully he'd only made it twenty miles outside the city when they arrested him.

Officers helped her to her feet and returned her gun which they found beside her. Evidently, they said, Terence pistol-whipped her then took off in his car, trying to evade arrest. As for the lump on her head, there was no "evidently" to it, she wanted to say. He *had* smashed her with her own gun and it damn well hurt.

The detective who coerced her to cooperate took her aside to update her. Initial investigation uncovered an area beneath the pier and beam house with a cage big enough to hold a large dog or small child. Terence kept his victim imprisoned in the cage with only water and minimal food. Having no way out, the girl was forced to defecate and urinate in the cage. With the amount of spoiled food and excrement, the detective noted, Terence kept more than one victim over several months.

While the detective described the horror below the house, investigators discovered Rachel's body. He'd bludgeoned her before burying her in a ready made grave in back of the house. Savannah couldn't bring herself to go near the house or hear any more details. Instead, her stomach revolted and, standing behind her cruiser, she threw up – nearby officers attributed it to heat and the hit on her head. Truth was Terence's aberrant nature and her inability to detect it wore on her conscience and stomach.

The autopsy later found dirt in the girl's lungs. Terence buried Rachel Ballard alive. Next to her, investigators discovered the decomposing remains of Carrie Duncan, a girl missing for eight months. She'd been dead for seven.

Savannah's mind kept replaying the patch of tilled soil behind

Terence's house. She should have known, her brain taunted. She should have known that area of ground was suspicious. She could have saved Rachel Ballard. Had she done something different, approached Terence another way or just flat out shot him dead, the little girl would have lived.

Through the miracle of Valium she survived testifying at Terence's trial. She took one before court convened and answered questions without allowing her vision to stray to the defendant's table. She held her gaze on the lawyers and the gallery, the latter filled to capacity with reporters and fellow officers.

Viewing the crime scene photos during the proceedings took its toll. Identifying Rachel Ballard's lifeless little body traumatized her beyond her wildest nightmares. Images of the girl lying in the grave drove Savannah to drink again. Rachel's pleading eyes surfaced at odd times during the day and especially nighttime. Savannah resorted to coping the only way she knew how. She threw back another shot of bourbon to erase the horrific scenes. The images only faded but never disappeared completely.

At the conclusion of the trial, after the guilty verdict and the sentence, Terence scanned the gallery for his partner. Savannah sat directly behind the district attorney and when her blue eyes met his hard glare, a chill raked her spine. The bailiff escorted Terence away in cuffs but not before he leaned into the aisle vowing, "You're dead, Prince. I'm coming for you and I'll kill you."

13

"Riverside Cemetery. Find a crypt with the name Lindsey and go inside.
Your next clue is there. You have fifteen minutes."

      Savannah's throat convulsed and her mouth went cotton dry. A
crypt in a cemetery. As evidenced by the note, the guy – Terence she
now assumed – knew very well about her claustrophobia. Diagnosed
later in her teenage years with clinical claustrophobia, Savannah found
any small area or room stifling. If she lingered too long in a small
enclosed place, her heart raced and her lungs seemed to shrink to half
their normal size. Breathing became so laborious she gasped for air as if
an invisible force smothered her. Her body literally rioted against her,
sweating, shaking and fighting for precious air – all while her mind
conjured images of an impending slow and painful death. Reason flew
out the window, common sense evaporated and threads of her sanity
gradually unwound while she spiraled into an all-encompassing panic to
survive.

      The old fear crept in slow but strong, wrapping her in the cold
terror of her childhood. Stopping the old memories proved futile.
Georgia and Seth were helping Grandpa pick peaches in the orchards – at

five, Savannah was too young, according to him – so she wandered the orchards looking for something to do. When a group of boys strolled by that she knew, she followed them to an old, rundown house down the road. She recalled how the sunlight streamed through the slats in the roof and walls, and how lonely it looked sitting back from the road in the middle of the tall wild grass – but she went along anyway.

Before she realized what happened, Savannah found herself locked in a tiny closet, bearing the insults and taunts older kids heaped on an unwanted tagalong child. She kicked and beat on the door, trying to dislodge it, to free herself. However, between their laughs and gibes, the boys trapped her by shoving old rotting furniture in front of the door.

Reacting to the memory, Savannah wiped her brow, recalling how damn hot it was that day many years ago. Her skin felt sticky with sweat and her clothes plastered to her body, her hair to her scalp. The smell of old musty wood permeated her senses. The reality of isolation overwhelmed her. Savannah had forced the hot, humid air into her lungs but found herself beginning to hyperventilate. She was going to die there as sure as she felt things crawling around her and on her. Brash little creatures with small tickling legs marching all over her, sending her sanity to the brink. Like the panic, the darkness sank to her bones. She had been there for hours, fighting off the insects and rodents and spent most of the time screaming, pushing and pounding on the door, praying someone would find her. She'd screamed so hard and long her voice gave out. Surely Georgia would miss her. Even as annoying as Savannah could be sometimes, Georgia would still miss her. Wouldn't she? And Seth – he looked after both girls with a protective nature of a father. He would look for her, wouldn't he?

After what seemed an eternity, she heard movement outside the door and the beam of a flashlight sweeping the darkness. Her voice, reduced to tremulous whimpers, called once more for her sister and brother. The heavy blockade was shoved aside like a feather. The walls shook as someone yanked hard on the door. Once it opened, through the falling dust, Savannah's tear-streaked face looked up at Georgia and Seth. Her sister reached down to embrace her but Savannah jumped into her arms and held on with a death grip. Seth and Georgia both stood for countless minutes calming her hysterical crying, and asking who'd locked her inside. Through sobs of misery, Savannah named the boys. Anger swept across her fourteen year-old brother's face and he balled his fists, promising, "I'll take care of 'em for ya, sis."

A diplomat at the tender age of eleven, Georgia suggested, "Don't kill 'em, Seth, but maim 'em real good."

And Seth had. He'd beaten the boys until his knuckles were bruised and chafed. He'd returned later that evening with a confident wink for Georgia and smile and hug for Savannah.

Now as she drove to the cemetery, Savannah calmed her breathing only to feel her heart pound harder inside her chest. How would she survive the trauma of being inside a *crypt* even a few seconds? "Fear makes the wolf bigger than he is," she mumbled. Georgia recited the old German proverb to her when she saw her sister stumbling for courage to which Savannah countered, "If we're supposed to hang around and be brave, why do we have legs and feet?"

"To kick the crap out of the person who scared us in the first place," Georgia inevitably answered.

And that was it, she decided. *Get busy and save Lindsey.* The thought brought to mind the five motives for murder. Fear, jealousy, money, revenge and protecting someone a person loves. "You shouldn't have screwed with my family, Terence," she grumbled while gripping the steering wheel. "You should have left them alone and only come after me."

As she drove up to Riverside Cemetery, she tamped down the ever mounting fear. She hated cemeteries anyway but being there at night made it worse. She drove through the open iron gates searching for signs of movement. Surely someone tended the place at night – she hoped. The thought of being the only living person in a vast sea of deceased ones downright "creepified" her, as Grandpa Prince always said. Adding to her fears – after passing the office she saw no lights on, no movement inside. She *was* alone.

After parking the car, she opened the door to a thick wave of icy humidity. The moonless night cast an eerie, almost unbearable atmosphere for her level of fear. What gnawed at her was the kidnapper's plan for the final note. What happened then?

She briefly analyzed her circumstances. She quite possibly could be walking into a situation where she died without facing the kidnapper – without having a chance to save Lindsey. Bad guys never played by the rules. He could have planted explosives in the crypt or could be waiting outside with a gun or knife once she exited the building. Getting a grasp on her gut feelings proved impossible. How could she rely on her gut instinct when it was always in a turmoil?

The sound of leaves rustling in the breeze served only to reinforce her panic. From the street she'd noticed only a few crypts in the cemetery so it wouldn't take long to locate the correct one. The challenge was *going inside* to retrieve the note. Starting at one end, she swept the flashlight's beam across every name she passed. At the fourth building, the stream of light revealed large block letters "Lindsey". She lowered the beam to the doors, unpleasantly surprised to observe the heavy iron gates woven with intricate iron filigree bars. It was a tight pattern that left little room for light to penetrate or for her to breathe if those doors swung shut.

Savannah glanced around her, searching for any soul tending the cemetery at this late hour. She saw nothing. Taking a deep breath, she cautiously opened one door and swept the flashlight across the room. No one hid or lingered inside so she opened the other door. By God, if she had to endure going inside this place, she'd do it with both doors wide open. Maybe she could breathe a little easier that way.

She stepped up one, two then up the third stair into the crypt. The stifling air hung stale and heavy as she stepped inside. The walls felt ice cold when she steadied herself with her hand. Glancing around the small stuffy room, she tried to locate the note fast. Savannah could feel her heart shifting into high gear the further she wandered into the crypt. Visions of the closet many years before flashed in her mind, forcing her to shove them aside. She *had* to find the note to save Lindsey. Failure was not an option.

At the far wall, a small stone bench caught her eye. Sweeping the flashlight's beam across it, she saw what looked like an envelope sitting on top.   Sucking in a deep breath, Savannah then scrambled to the bench, praying she retrieved it before she lost her mind.

One hand laid upon the note when a noise outside spun her around, the flashlight in one hand, her weapon in the other, "Who's there?"   Silence followed the shaky inquiry.   *Well, if they didn't know you were scared out of your mind, they do now.*   Shoring up her courage, she tried again, "Come on out.   I'm a police officer, I'm armed and at this point, very willing to shoot."   Better, but not entirely convincing. Still no one came from the shadows.

Savannah felt herself shaking.   Discharging a gun inside the small room wouldn't be prudent but she was scared.   Sweat formed along her body and it only made her shivering worse.   Finally, she wheeled around to the note – she'd grab it and run.   Her hand closed on the note just as the same noise appeared again.   This time when she turned, however, a tall wide-shouldered figure stood at the doors.   Dressed in black and a ski mask, his vision locked on hers as his hands worked swiftly and efficiently with the iron doors to close them.   Then Savannah heard it.   The sound of a chain being looped through the handles.

Total panic took over and she dropped the flashlight while racing to the doors.   The room went pitch black when the flashlight hit the concrete floor and just before reaching the doors, she kicked at them, giving her leg all the power and leverage she could.   The blow knocked the shadow backward a step but he quickly returned to his work.

Savannah snaked her fingers through the small holes in the doors, "Let me out!"   She heard a low chuckle from the man and she kicked at the doors again.   "No!" she screamed, finally realizing how her paranoia undermined her common sense. She'd forgotten to bring the cell phone with her. She was alone and chained inside a small room – no, a *crypt* – with no one to help her.

Terror threatened to commandeer her senses. The man smiled behind the ski mask. She shouldered the doors, hoping to dislodge them and knowing it was impossible. The chain gave a little, the padlock clanged against the iron doors. He'd wrapped the chain repeatedly through the handles to reinforce its strength.

Savannah found herself preaching at the top of her lungs, "Terence, let me out! I know you, you want me to suffer but you don't want me to die in here!"

The man stopped smiling. He approached the doors and as he climbed the stairs, his body blocked the dim light outside and threw her into a dizzying blackness. She stared into the dark shadow of his face as he whispered, "It's your decision if you lose your mind in there. Personally I'd love to stay and watch if you did. If your paranoia kills you, fine. Just remember Lindsey is in capable, *very* loving hands."

Savannah had no trouble seeing his smile as he backed away from the crypt. Shouldering the irons gates proved useless. She grasped the bars with an intensity that could have bent them. She tried to control the urge to hyperventilate but still her words heaved out with labored breaths, "You want to kill me yourself. You want to kill me with your bare hands, don't you? Let me out and we'll see who wins the fight."

His head tilted as if contemplating her speech. The sound of her straining for air seemed to delight him however and he shrugged, "I think we know who will win. If you remember, I was driving away while

Officer Prince's lights were still out. You see, Savannah, I'm not choosy. As long as you die, that's my only goal. How you die doesn't matter." The same smile emerged and he waved, "Bye-bye now."

As he turned, she smashed the door with her fist, hoping to reach out and grab him. Instead, she whimpered as pain ripped through her knuckles and up her arm. The pattern on the iron door prevented her from reaching out, the hurting reminded. She was locked very well inside. "Terence!" she screamed and kicked at the doors. "Come back! Be a man and face me!" She heard the solitary sound of her ex-partner walking through the grass – leaving her confined in the tiny hell of the crypt. She nailed the door again with her fist, "You coward! Come back!" Her heart pounded in her chest and her ears, the blood coursing through the latter in a deafening roar.

Memories of her childhood descended on her in cold horrifying waves. Alone with no one aware of her location. No cell phone to call out. No human within hearing range of her calls for help. The finality of the situation hit full force and she sank to her knees, tears coming to her eyes, "No," she pleaded in a tremulous whisper. "Not again."

Georgia wasn't coming. Neither was Seth. This time it was up to her. Lindsey needed her but the walls of the crypt shrank in, the air grew thicker. Savannah sucked in a deep breath to stay calm. The beaded sweat on her brow trickled down, stinging her eyes. She wiped it away with the back of her hand. "Gotta be a way out of here," her quivering voice assured. Her tongue swept her lips only to notice her chin trembling as harshly as her voice. "Try to calm down and think." Trying to focus wasn't working yet. The struggle for oxygen became her main objective. It felt like an elephant sat on her chest, preventing her lungs from expanding and that alone rooted the panic deeper.

Feeling faint, Savannah was surprised when the recollection of a note overwhelmed the fear. Scrambling across the cold, dusty floor, she felt around blindly for the flashlight. She switched it on and flashed the beam across the small room to the stone bench. Ripping the note open took a second – reading the words took longer because each one slid home like a knife between the ribs. "This is the end game. I win, you lose. Lindsey stays with me, at least until she ceases to be useful. The way I see it, you have two choices: One, suffer the agony of going insane inside here which wouldn't be pleasant at all. Scream all you want but as you noticed, no one's around to hear you. No one, not even the maintenance crew, will find you for several hours so you'll have plenty of time to choke on your terror. Or you can end your misery by placing the barrel of your gun in your mouth and pulling the trigger. Your choice."

Tears streamed down her cheeks, mingled with sweat and dropped onto the note. Crumpling it in her fist, Savannah threw it across the room and scrambled for the doors again. Frantically she kicked them and beat them with her fists until she saw the faint sheen of blood covering her knuckles. "Let me out! Help!" she grabbed the doors and rattled them, hoping to jar them loose. A sudden noise behind her startled her and she spun. Images crept back of mice and spiders crawling on her in the hot, musty closet. She sucked in shallow, quick gasps until she found herself clinging to the iron gates, straining for fresh cool air. "Mama, help me," she cried between labored breaths. "Help me find a way out." She swiped her tears away again, "You're the only one who knows where I am. Please help me."

It had been years since she'd been reduced to a sniveling heap of tears, especially to this humiliating degree. If she didn't watch herself, she'd descend back to that desperate young girl locked in the closet, with terror ravaging her physical control and robbing her mental capabilities. Panic to that extent defiled a person's dignity and stripped them of all that they had become, reverting them to a scared child not even comforted by their prayers and tears. *Georgia... Seth... Ennis... Anyone, please...* Savannah stood paralyzed, silently calling for family, friends and even strangers to happen by and see her – or at least her car parked out front.

To survive until daylight meant nothing – Lindsey would be dead by then. Terence was right in his first note. Seth would never forgive Savannah for failing. That didn't matter as much as Savannah couldn't forgive *herself* if something happened to her niece.

She withdrew her weapon, lifted it to her vision and studied it in the soft moonlight. *You have two choices. Stay and lose your mind with the knowledge you failed your whole family, especially Lindsey, or you can bite down on the barrel and pull the trigger.* A drop of sweat rolled down the bridge of her nose while another angled into the corner of her eye. She was blinking back the burning sensation when she caught sight of a possible solution. Feeling her mother's strength flood her, she stopped to listen to the quiet assurance and comfort Charlene's spirit offered. Her mother reminded her that neither of the stated choices was acceptable. First, she couldn't sit by and watch Terence take off with Lindsey and two, Charlene sternly lectured from beyond, Savannah was too damn stubborn to shoot herself. Her daughters, Charlene pointed out very clearly, were *not* wired to give up or give in. Savannah nodded. Her family was too important to her and her niece was depending on her. She herself might not survive the ordeal but she'd do her damnedest to make sure Lindsey did.

She covered one ear with her free hand and shrugged her shoulder against the other ear. Then she aimed the gun at the lock outside, took a deep breath and pulled the trigger. The resulting blast not only set her back a step but literally rattled her brain. Pain reverberated in her ears and a sharp metallic odor wafted into her nostrils. The lock moved but damned if she heard it clank against the doors due to the strong ringing still lingering in her ears.

Savannah poked two then managed three fingers between the filigree in the door. Just enough to feebly grab the lock like a crab using its pinchers. She pulled on it then felt it slide through her hold and bang against the door.

Again she reached for it and yanked, but the lock stayed true. "Damn," she mumbled, then shouldered a traveling bead of sweat away from her cheek. She aimed the weapon as best she could, plugged her ears and shot. Savannah swore the second shot burst her eardrums. The pain was worse and nausea churned her stomach from the adrenaline and hurting. Swallowing it back, she gave the lock a warning through clenched teeth, "You'll come open if I have to gnaw through the damn doors."

Squeezing her fingers through again, she latched onto the sturdy silver lock and yanked hard. It slipped free of her hold and clanged the door with a solid chime. Savannah just stood and stared at it. Using the back of her hand, she swept another budding drop of perspiration from her brow and sighed. *Two shots frittered away – three counting the one Randy wasted. My ears can't stand another so what am I going to do?* She sagged against the wall to regroup her thoughts. The concrete began closing in on her and she fought to retain her fragile control. She combed through her hair and winced as the salty sweat stung her wounded knuckles. Then she heard it.

Something besides the wind lurked outside. Dried leaves flew past as the breeze picked up into a full fledged wind. The cold front forecast for the next day was early. The weathermen predicted snow – not much – but if it was cold enough to snow it was cold enough to turn her into a Savannah-sicle before daybreak.

The cold didn't affect her as much as the soft sweeping sound of shoes against dead grass. She lifted her .38, leveled it at the door. Another noise, this one like a whisper came from just outside. A moment passed when she heard it again, this time the whisper turned to a gravelly male voice, "Hey, Prince."

Savannah reinforced her hold on the gun, "Who's there?"

"Knowing you, you've got your damn gun pointed straight at the door. I'm here to help but if you're gonna shoot me, I won't."

A spark of hope finally sped her heart for a joyful reason. Judging by the phrasing, she knew who stood outside, "Riley, is that you?"

"No, it's your grandma. Now, you gonna shoot me if I come around the corner?"

She holstered the gun and scrambled to the doors, her hands

trembling as the fingers threaded through the filigree, "Riley, get me out of here. I'm losing it."

"Yeah, no shit. Still trying to shoot your way out of situations. I imagine your mama was grateful you weren't armed before birth. You holstered that gun yet?"

"Yeah, yeah," she answered impatiently. The moment she saw the round shadow step into the moonlight, she sucked in a deep breath. Help was here. Riley would save her. "Please hurry, Murph. I'm dying," the desperation in her tone hadn't quite hit her.

Riley, however, picked up on it instantly, "Settle down. I remember you got problems with little places. That's why I wanted your gun put away. If you shot me, I'd never let you live it down."

Savannah appraised her burly ex-partner. Always the epitome of calm, no matter how wild or dangerous the situation became. He coped with his stress with dark humor but Savannah found his sense of humor charming most times. Even while tangling with the stubborn lock, Riley's chubby, ruddy face showed only concentration of the task at hand. He glanced at her and his expression changed at the panic in her features, "Calm down, Savannah. Close your eyes and take deep breaths. I ain't answering to Rutherford if you keel over on my watch."

She followed his directions and as he spoke, she felt twenty-one again. Hearing the roughness of Murphy's voice and his stern directions brought her back to when she worried more about making the quota of speeding tickets than surviving a hell like this night. Riley Murphy was a tough, capable man not only in body but character and she took that moment to absorb some of his strength. "Murph?" his name shuddered

from her lips as she squeezed her eyes shut tight. She heard the chain
rattle against the door as he worked.

"Yeah?"

"Thanks for saving me."

She heard him grunt then sigh, "Prince, you really are a head
case. *The whole department* knew where you were. Rutherford about
pissed his pants when he found out you were in a cemetery. We waited
to make our move so your niece would be safe. You don't normally find
me dressed as a groundskeeper, you know." The sound of the chain
clattering through the handles caught her attention.

Riley waited then asked, "Well, you movin' in or comin' out?"

Savannah opened her eyes to see the chain gone. A few steps
back, dressed in tan overalls stood Murphy, a huge bolt cutter dangling
from one large fist. He swung it out to his side, motioning for her to
come out. She gladly pushed the doors wide and scurried into the cold
night air. Immediately her lungs released and relaxed. Without
thinking, she flung her arms around Riley, startling him, "Whoa, are we
getting married or something?"

At that moment hugging Riley was similar to embracing a giant
teddy bear. Big, soft and warm. With her arms still secure around his
ample chest, she kissed his cheek, "Right about now, I'd agree to nearly
anything. Thanks for getting me out."

He chuckled and hugged her back, "Hey, it's just another gold
star in my file. Anytime, kiddo. Just be careful. If this guy knows your
weaknesses – and he does – he's more dangerous than you think."

Savannah tightened her embrace, "You *do* still love me, don't you?"

He patted her back and broke with their usual tradition, "You know I do. You're still a pain in *my* ass and I'm still wiping *yours* but you know I love you."

Her laugh trembled as badly as her body. Leave it to Murphy to tell it straight out. Somehow, though, she sensed he was sincerely worried about her. His parting words proved it, "Now don't go dying on me, ya hear?"

14

Damp and sticky with cold perspiration, Savannah jogged to the Camaro. In reality, it was more like loping considering her weariness peaked and adrenaline bottomed out. What did she do now? Terence obviously hadn't expected her to escape from the crypt. There were no other notes and now she ran to her car, freezing to death in the cold blustery wind with no location to find, no deadline to meet, no idea where her niece was. She muttered an expletive guaranteed to mortify anyone nearby. Had her mother been alive, Savannah was sure she would have slapped her for saying it.

She rounded the side of the car and got in to cut the biting wind off of her. Her vision went to the cell phone sitting in the passenger's seat. She should call Seth and find a way to break the news. *Hi, Seth. I really screwed up...* Then what? "I'm sorry" just wasn't enough and sounded so... empty. So pathetic. *Your daughter is probably dead...* She couldn't bear to think it, much less say the words aloud. *She's dead because of my weakness and stupidity to be caught in a trap.*

Her eyes squeezed shut, her teeth clenched hard in an attempt to evict the words from her mind. The images, though, introduced a fresh, all encompassing torment she'd not experienced before – one she was sure would haunt her to her dying breath. The image of Lindsey reaching for her, calling for her, then as the realization slowly dawned that Aunt Savannah wasn't coming, tears began flowing, her screams of desperation evolving to terror as Terence approached.

Savannah shook free of the bizarre video running in her tired mind. Wrapping her fingers around the phone she noticed it felt different. Bringing it closer, she turned it over. Taped to the back of the phone was a folded piece of paper. Praying it might be another clue, she switched on the dome light. The note had her name scribbled across it and she peeled it away from the cell. Her body still shivered from nerves, sweat and cold which made opening the note a hefty challenge.

"If you're reading this, you've managed only to prolong the inevitable. Find your way to the roof of the Madison Tower and you'll also find your way to Lindsey. She'll be near the air conditioning units. The rules are: One, you arrive before 5:00 a.m. – at 5:01 I take her and leave. Two, you climb the stairs to the roof – no elevators. Three, leave your car behind and find another way to the building. This is the last note you'll receive."

Savannah's heart jump started again, hammering relentlessly in her chest. She still had hope but did she have time? Her watch read 3:02 a.m. With luck, she could squeak by. All she needed was a cab. *Yeah, right. In this part of town at this time of night.* Flipping through her mind's rolodex, she located a cab company relatively close and dialed information for the number. Once she had a ride lined up she sat back to rest. The Madison Tower – one of the tallest in Atlanta – loomed over downtown with fifty floors of mirrored glass. Running those flights of stairs would kill her. The knee she injured while playing high school golf rarely bothered her unless she overexerted it. Fifty floors of climbing and it would be screaming at her. The mere thought of it shot pangs through her leg. She just hoped it held up long enough to save Lindsey.

o   o   o

Savannah thanked the cab driver for his lightning fast efforts. After seeing her badge and hearing her story, the driver floored the cab for most of the way. Trying to gather her thoughts and plans proved useless as they rounded corners at high rates of speed and flew through the sparsely populated Atlanta streets. They drove up to the Madison Tower, her watch read 3:30. She knew she'd need every minute to ascend the monstrous building.

After exiting the cab, she approached the building with trepidation and awe. Completed in the last two years, the Madison Tower was diamond-shaped from above and with its mirrored glass sides, Savannah always considered the place too ostentatious for Atlanta's skyline. But, as she was discovering, her city was still capable of surprising her.

Staring fifty floors up to the roof of the giant, she prayed Lindsey was there. She also prayed the child wasn't too fearful of heights. According to the note, her niece could be found on the roof near the air conditioning units.

Throwing open the building's door, she noted the place looked more like a swanky hotel than an office building from marble floors and dark paneled walls to the reception kiosk and guard station, both crafted from mahogany wood. She expected to see a security guard leaned back in his chair fighting off the urge to nap. With her badge at the ready, she searched for the guard but was surprised when the desk stood vacant. A fleeting concern furrowed her brow. A place like the Madison Tower had to employ security because they'd be stupid not to but that particular night she wasn't about to argue.

Pocketing the badge, she turned her attention to finding the stairs. The empty reception area felt slightly eerie with its minimal lighting, and in a darkened corner she found the stairway sign.

Beginning the colossal climb, Savannah charged up the stairs. Even the most intensive workout paled in comparison to climbing each story stair by stair. Her knee, as she fully expected, fired white hot bolts of pain to her toes and hip. Her energy level sapped quickly after the first twenty floors, the muscles in her legs burned and her chest heaved to catch her breath. *This is what he wants,* she thought. *For me to be tired and vulnerable to an attack.* She reached back for her weapon and checked it while taking a moment's rest. Stealing a glance at her watch, she noted the time: 3:59.

She alternated between climbing and essentially hopping the last thirty flights of stairs, allowing her left knee to bear the brunt of the weight. Each time she settled on her right one, a stifled groan filled the stairway and tears gathered in her eyes. The last flight forced her to use the railing to aid in the climb. Now only a door stood between her and Lindsey – if her niece was truly there. Savannah wouldn't put it past

Terence to lie just to trap her.

Savannah willed herself to continue for the child's sake. He may have been waiting for Savannah on the roof but she intended to save her niece before he jumped her.

Finally, she reached the top floor with a few minutes to spare. She leaned on her knees to catch her breath before opening the door. The word *exhaustion* paled in comparison to how she felt. At that moment she was grateful she applied to the police and not the fire department years ago. She couldn't handle climbing like firefighters had to with the equipment they carried. She only carried a .38 and was positively drained.

Opening the door leading outside, she gasped when the cold wind struck her like a slap across the face. At the same time, it renewed her energy somewhat, cleared her head. Though they felt weak and wobbly, the pain in her legs ebbed slightly and her lungs found welcome control instead of the arduous huffing and puffing she'd done for a solid twenty floors.

Savannah reached back to withdraw her weapon from its holster. Navigating the roof would be a nightmare because of the huge air conditioning units. Circular in shape, they stood several feet taller than her which made it impossible to see around them in the blackness. Calling out to Lindsey seemed the right idea but she held off. If the girl was there, Savannah would find her eventually.

Softly treading over the asphalt roof, Savannah peered around an air conditioning unit. Nothing came into view in the darkness. Shadows rose from the other units and buildings nearby, disorienting her. She tiptoed around one unit to another, trying to focus on objects illuminated by the moonlight and distant lights. She blinked, trying to focus and orient herself to the surroundings.

She stayed away from ledges simply to keep her sanity. If she allowed herself to think about where she was, both she and Lindsey were doomed. Stepping between two shadowed walls of air conditioning units, something to her right moved and Savannah wheeled. Her gun leveled at a faint silhouette next to the ledge of the building. Nearing inch by inch, she realized the silhouette stood shorter than an adult and much shorter than Terence. From the darkness came a tremulous whisper, "Aunt Savannah? Is that you?"

Savannah's initial reaction was to collapse – however the danger of Terence lurking nearby shelved that idea. Instead, she drew a deep breath and swallowed what felt like her heart. Lindsey was cold but seemed okay.

Savannah holstered her gun and as she neared Lindsey, images of Rachel Ballard flashed in her mind. Terence bound her niece in much the same way Savannah saw Rachel years earlier, only instead of being tied to a railing inside his house, Lindsey's wrists were bound to a railing fifty stories above the city.

Purging the memory, she tried to comfort Lindsey who began crying the instant Savannah stepped into the soft moonlight. She worked with the rope binding her niece to the ledge's railing, "Shh, baby," she whispered to her. "I wanna get you out of here before he comes back." Terence never left, she knew that, but to settle the hysterical little girl, Savannah had to convince her otherwise.

She peered down the building's sheer drop and her stomach clenched. Swallowing again, she was calmed somewhat when Lindsey's arms wrapped tightly around her waist. Savannah held on to her, savoring the moment while trying to warm and calm her. Tears fell down Lindsey's cheeks when she snuggled against her aunt, begging, "I want to go home." A brief memory appeared in Savannah's mind of her speaking those very words to R.J. after Bryan tried to molest her. There'd been no comparison to the relief she felt when wrapping her arms around her father, knowing everything would be all right. Now *she* was the protector – the person deemed the savior of the moment. Nothing felt better than this...

The cold wind suddenly picked up and whipped around them. Savannah removed her jacket and draped it around Lindsey's shoulders, whispering, "Then let's go home. You've been a brave girl, sweetheart." *A lot more courageous than I am, for sure,* she thought. She lifted the girl into her arms and felt a sense of relief when Lindsey's arms hugged her neck and her legs locked around Savannah's waist like a vise.

She stroked the girl's hair, whispering to her as they made their way to the door. She reached for the knob when a steady pressure registered at the base of her skull. Startled, she froze as the voice behind her instructed, "Put the girl down. We're not done."

She watched Lindsey glance over her shoulder and pure fear coursed through her tear-filled vision. She held tighter to Savannah, refusing to let go. Before his appearance, Lindsey's sobbing ebbed to sniffling and muted whimpers. When Terence emerged from the shadows, the young girl clamped down tight on Savannah's hips and neck, her face turned to hide from Terence. That worried Savannah but Lindsey's crying heightened to hysterical proportions which alarmed her even more with fears he'd violated the girl.

She shushed Lindsey, trying to calm her down. Without turning, Savannah tried to reason with Terence, "It's me you want. Let the child go."

The pressure on the gun mounted, the grasp trembled, "I said put her down now."

Savannah knew there was no other way to save Lindsey. She whispered in the girl's ear then tried to pry her legs and arms from around her. The child still refused to let go.

Terence nudged the gun barrel against the back of Savannah's head as a silent motivation for her to immediately comply. Lindsey, though, was positively terrified and Savannah said as much, "Give me a second, will you? She's scared." Again she whispered to her niece, this time trying to instill the importance of what she was saying. Sniffing back tears between the sobs, Lindsey finally nodded. Savannah patted her back, "Good girl."

Kneeling to set the child down, Savannah waited until Lindsey's feet touched the ground before yanking the door open, "Run!"

Responding to the command, the girl bolted through the doorway, her weeping fading into the distance as the door closed. When Savannah told her she was proud of her and she needed to be brave just a little longer, her words evidently bolstered Lindsey. As fast as the girl ran down the stairs, Savannah figured her for a future track star.

She began to stand when something heavy – she assumed it was

Terence's foot – collided with her back and launched her face first against the door. It felt like a bomb exploded inside her head. The blow incapacitated her temporarily, sending her flat to the asphalt.

From the corner of her eye, she saw Terence step closer. His shoes scraped the asphalt with the languor of a person taking their time, planning their next attack. Hoping she had enough time and strength to stand, she pulled a knee up to begin the laborious process. Instead, a ramming pain tore through her side like a freight train, overwhelming her senses and stole her breath. A second blow expelled a cry that ultimately faded to a mere whimper. Savannah knew she had to get up. She had to stand or Terence would gladly beat her to death and she refused to go down without fighting.

The instant she hoisted her aching body to its elbows, another crippling assault flattened her again. She arched against the throbbing only to suffer an additional vicious kick. This time she heard the full fledged scream pour from her lips. Her brain implored her to fight back somehow or merely deflect his foot from mauling her. Her body, though, still reeled in the sudden, brutal attacks. Speaking proved futile as any attempt materialized in a groan or whimper. Turning over seemed not only monumental but useless. Terence would kick or punch any part of her available. Right now he concentrated on her back – if she turned over, he'd break her jaw or worse.

He braced his foot on the back of her neck while retrieving her gun, "You won't need this anymore so I'll keep it. Put your hands behind you."

Still trying to wear off the brutal blows to her back and kidneys,

Savannah sniffed back the tears threatening to fall. She whimpered at the pressure he applied to her neck.

"You always were a tough bitch," he said. "Why do you think I had you running around all night? Besides making you pay, I wanted some of that fight outta you." He dug his heel in harder, "Hands behind you *now*."

Hoping he'd lighten the pressure on her neck, she complied. He jerked the handcuffs from her belt and a moment later she felt the cold metal compress around each wrist. "You hold me responsible for your conviction," she said, "but you're a sick, twisted asshole, Terence. Prison is where you belong."

"And Hell is where you belong, *partner*." He fisted her hair and dragged her to her knees. Pain engulfed her from head to toe while she struggled to her knees. Gnashing her teeth against the throbbing, Savannah watched him pace in front of her. She half expected a boot up her chin the way he stalked slowly back and forth.

"At least you were supposed to be my partner. Too bad you turned traitor." He sounded strangely calm as he spoke. He lazily sauntered closer. "And you know what happens to traitors," his fingers threaded her hair and fisted again, this time he wrenched her head back. "Look at me, Savannah. I want you to see what you did to me."

Tears blinded her. The pain in her back radiated throughout her body and now he forced her head back so far the muscles stretched to their limits. She really didn't want to face Terence. The venom in his voice alone was lethal. If his actions were a taste of her future, she dreaded it worse than dying.

A determined jerk on her hair opened her eyes. When she looked up, she saw him grinning at her. Terence's normal smile appeared insidious enough but when enraged, the smile brought a whole new definition to the term evil. It gave him a meaner appearance if that was possible. Dark eyes drilled into a square face, a strong jaw set hard, and a narrow, lipless mouth that gave him a feral look especially when he smiled.

A sting against the side of her neck widened her eyes with the realization he held a knife just under her ear. Where he stored the gun, she wasn't sure. A brief glance around her didn't reveal any answers. She assumed he, like Randy had earlier, put it in his back pocket.

Terence pressed harder on the blade until she flinched. His voice softened to a whisper, "Do you know what they do to cops in prison?"

Looking into the cold, pitiless pools, she shivered. An abyss of evil stared back at her, making her body shake all over. If she held any hopes about surviving, his murderous expression cured them. His features reinforced the fact she wouldn't be going home alive. She knew the brutality of this man, his capabilities and his bitterness toward her. Terence LaVeau *would* kill her. The questions were how and how long would he make her suffer.

"Answer me!" he demanded.

"Yes, I know what they do to cops in prison," she replied. The blade dug in and she cringed. "Especially the ones who molest kids."

His grin widened in a familiar way – a way that didn't bode well. She'd seen the smile at the trial when they escorted him away in handcuffs.

Through gnashed teeth he finished, "You're gonna wish you'd never testified against me, Prince. We were partners." He leaned in, "We were supposed to protect each other."

"Not when my partner molests and kills children." She saw it coming and couldn't stop it. He let go and just as quickly, his foot reared back and sped toward her. The debilitating blow to her stomach wrenched a cry from her as she crumpled on the roof. She couldn't stop her tears.

Terence stood over her, the gun now in his hand. He leveled it until the muted light faintly glinted off the metal. She was staring straight down the barrel as he ordered her to sit up.

Convincing her body to move took enormous effort. When she turned her head, everything spun. Savannah closed her eyes, praying the merry-go-round might slow down. She struggled to her side and with enough effort, she finally made it to her knees again.

"Do you remember their names?"

His question brought forth the painful memories of the trial and of seeing Rachel Ballard's pleading eyes. Pretty Rachel with her long, shining brown hair and charismatic smile. Eyes as blue as wild lupine, the girl in the school picture exhibited a true beauty waiting to emerge in later years. She was tall for her age and, according to her mother, loved playing basketball. Carrie Duncan's flaxen hair and freckled cheeks appeared next. Green eyes the color of apples seemed to smile at the school photographer. The small gold-rimmed glasses perched on her nose gave the image of a studious child and even at the tender age of seven, as her mother attested to, she loved to read.

Their images transformed in Savannah's mind. The crime scene photos haunted her from the time she'd seen them. From the crime scene photo's vantage point, Rachel Ballard's fetal position and her closed eyes gave her a deceptively peaceful look but Savannah knew the child suffered. The blows incapacitated her but, being buried alive, death was slow and painful. By the time police photographed her, a blue tinge began spreading along her extremities and her skin developed a waxy appearance. And Carrie Duncan's remains were just that. She'd been dead long enough only hair and bones remained.

Terence found Savannah's hesitation amusing, "Don't tell me you forgot already. You really are a heartless bitch, aren't you?"

If she could free herself, he'd certainly find out how heartless and cruel she could be. Savannah was about to answer when a sudden recollection gave her an idea. When Bobby retrieved her cuffs from Randy he handed the key to her and she stuffed the handcuff key in her pant's pocket. Cautiously, she slid her fingers into the pocket as Terence replaced the gun with the knife again. He yanked her head back and nestled the blade against the pulse beneath her right ear. A stinging sensation registered as he pressed it deeper, nicking the flesh. Savannah squirmed at the pressure, trying to pull away.

"Their names," he demanded. "Say their names, Prince."

Freeing herself quietly was the trick. So far she'd managed to slide the key in one cuff and carefully twisted. The bracelet opened silently. If she could swing at him or, at the very least, defend herself, she stood a decent chance. She switched hands with the key as she answered, "Rachel Ballard and Carrie Duncan."

Terence nodded, almost impressed with the recollection. He stepped closer, delaying her from freeing her other hand. "They were sweet things," his voice sang with a touch of sadness. He bent down, whispering in her ear, "Almost as sweet as Lindsey."

The declaration focused her sharper than the knife at her throat. Each syllable's impact hit with more force than his feet or fists. A sickness rose in her belly as a tempest stirred inside her, "What did you say?"

Terence elaborated with malicious glee, "You didn't honestly think I could resist that darling little morsel, did you? In my opinion, she's the icing on the cake."

She twisted the key in the handcuff, the bracelet swung open but Terence's fist tightened in her hair, the blade sank deeper, "She was so tempting when she looked up at me with those big beautiful eyes and since she means the world to you I treated her exceptionally well. The sweet thing, she kept saying no. Guess what I said? I told her Aunt Savannah said it was okay."

The mere thought of him touching her precious niece sent her into a rage. Mustering what power she retained, Savannah balled her fist and swung with every ounce of strength she possessed. Her knuckles collided with his crotch and Terence shrieked, dropped the knife and cradled his throbbing groin. She pulled her legs from beneath her, recoiled and smashed her heels against his grasping hands. Terence collapsed to his knees, crying out.

On her feet now, Savannah but purposefully stalked toward him. Terence revealed the very issue plaguing her for nearly twelve hours. In the most heinous manner, the most unspeakable way, he'd hurt one of the dearest people in her life. Now she directed her rage to killing Terence LaVeau, to send him to Hell. She wouldn't allow him to survive for trial this time.

Still cradling himself, Terence's vision lifted to hers in time to see her foot speeding toward his jaw. The blow knocked him backward onto his back. Standing over him, she ground the words between clenched teeth, "I told you, you miserable son of a bitch. If you touched her, I'd cut you into pieces." She bent to retrieve the knife. After she was done, she intended to stick around and watch Terence die. In her mind, the action couldn't be labeled as "murder". It equated to a rule of the Old South. When someone molested a child, they were disposed of like vermin. At present, Terence LaVeau sank way past vermin.

Savannah fisted the knife and swung back. His arm lifted to deflect the attack but the blade slashed the length of his forearm. Terence yelped and she sliced the knife through the air again, this time carving a trench down his arm from elbow to fingertips. She raised the knife again intending to end the confrontation once and for all. Midway through her downswing, Terence caught her wrist and twisted.

He pushed himself to his feet and used his strength and weight to bull her against the railing. Savannah scrambled to hold on as he bent her over the barrier. "And I told you," he reminded, "I'd see you dead. Looks like I win."

Writhing for one ounce of leverage, Savannah found herself – again – literally fighting for her life. Her head, back and stomach still killed her but, she reflected, it was strange how the aches disappeared when staring fifty stories down. Traffic along the streets remained light, the cars resembling a boy's Matchbox collection. The streetlights illuminated the target – the sidewalk next to the Madison Tower's entrance. If she failed to hang on to the railing and fight her way back onto the roof, she'd be chowder in a matter of seconds.

Terence's hand clamped around one ankle and began to hoist her over. Savannah held to the railing with all her strength. Then she kicked, blindly aiming for his face. Her foot landed against something solid and his fiery curse gave her hope that she gained a slight advantage. She reared back again. A loud noise followed by a searing pain ripped across her thigh, expelling a brief shriek from her lips. *What the hell just happened*, she cringed. The familiarity and amount of pain revealed the truth. She'd been shot. Again. *Damn it*, she complained to herself, *that's one time too many in a career.*

Through the blood roaring in her ears she heard another shot ring out but thankfully this one didn't find its way to her flesh. In the span of mere seconds, she reacted to the shots and realized the physical impossibility that Terence had done it. Both his hands were securely engaged at the moment trying to heave her over the edge of the building – and semi-succeeding at it. She was three quarters on the wrong side of Hell right now. One more decent shove and she'd be dangling over the side of the massive building.

Strangely, Terence's grasp on her and her ankle loosened then fell away. Whatever happened, she was grateful for the breather so she could regroup her strength and sanity. But, her wary mind prompted, they weren't alone on the roof. Someone, an *armed* someone, lingered in the shadows and they weren't afraid to shoot. Question was, who were they aiming at, Terence or her?

Before allowing herself to mire down in too many questions, she threw her leg back over the railing. Her other leg, thankfully uninjured, pushed her halfway over to the roof side. Then, as if straight out of Friday the 13th, another grasp wrapped around her ankle, a second hand grabbed at her waist. Assuming Terence recovered his balance, she reinforced her hold on the railing and kicked to rid herself of him once and for all.

"Oww!" a familiar voice cried. Now other anonymous hands pawed her clothes, wrists, anything to grasp and hold. "Cut it out, will ya?" the voice continued. "That's my nose you're aimin' at."

It couldn't be... Could it? "Ennis?" she called, praying it really was him.

"Glad you recognized me before you beat me to a pulp. You kick like Jackie Chan, girl."

Her fight instantly stopped, allowing him and another cop to help her over the railing to safety. Several flashlight beams swung back and forth across the roof, illuminating the immediate area around them. Besides Ennis, half a dozen cops surrounded her and Terence, some checking him, others attending to protocol and the remaining tended to her, as Ennis did.

She wanted to stand but her legs gave way the second they touched the ground. She slid down onto the roof, sitting and staring blankly at Terence's lifeless body next to her. It was honestly over. Thanks to Ennis, she'd survived Terence's promise to kill her and his near successful attempt to follow through.

Ennis kneeled beside her, his hand cupped her cheek to draw her vision to his, "Are you okay?"

She didn't know how to answer. Tears swelled as she threw her arms around her partner, "Thank you."

Ennis smiled a little, his arms enfolding her, "Well, I hope you still feel like thanking me once you find out I was the culprit who shot you."

Pulling away, she eyed him with slight disbelief, "You?"

He nodded sheepishly, "I panicked. I saw him about to toss you and when you kicked him, you got in my bullet's way."

Savannah saw the concern on his face. He was afraid she was pissed at him. Sniffing back tears, she laughed a little, "Well, at least you didn't aim for my ass. Then I would have wondered if you liked me."

Ennis switched on his flashlight to examine her bleeding thigh. The grazing wound, located two thirds up her outer thigh, eked more blood when he touched it, "Could have been much worse," he said, trying to put a positive spin on it. "My aim could have been six inches off."

Savannah forced a smile since it really wasn't funny at all. His fingers rested right about "six inches off" – nearly at her groin, "You shoot me there, partner, and there'll be a killin'." She wiped away the remains of some tears, "You're either a damn good shot or you need to visit the shooting range again. I'll choose the former."

An officer approached them, nodded at Savannah then addressed Ennis, "Found the security guard in a storage room. His throat was cut."

Ennis glanced at her evidently awaiting her reaction but she barely had enough energy to process her own name. He reached in his pocket for a handkerchief. Savannah could never understand him. Even on his worst days when he dressed one step above a transient, he still carried a hanky. She watched him moisten it with his tongue and reach toward her, assuring, "It's clean. I keep my blowin' rag in my other pocket."

So now he carries two, she thought, amused. She really wanted to kiss him. His tender touch as he cleaned blood from under her nose nearly brought another onslaught of tears. He was such a kind, gentle man with her. He doubled the hanky for a clean side then swept the lines of tears away, "There. What do you think we get you to the hospital now?"

She threw him a sideways glance, curious about his phrasing. Ennis shrugged, "I know you girls have to look perfect wherever you go. To me, you look like a dream come true but I figured you'd box my ears if I didn't clean you up a bit."

She elbowed him good-naturedly. Personally she didn't care if looked like she was pulled from a dung heap – which she was relatively sure she did – but Ennis was always thinking. That's why she liked him. Well, just one of the reasons...

Ennis leaned in to help her stand. Temptation got the best of her and she tugged him closer by the hand. A startled expression adorned his face and remained there as her lips met his. Once the surprise faded, he settled into the kiss. Oh yes, this definitely rated high on her scale of bliss. Ennis's resolve seemed to melt along with hers as his fingers traced her jaw and cupped the back of her head. The kiss lingered a moment longer then she parted with a long sigh.

Still mere inches from her lips, he inquired, "I'm certainly not complaining but what was that for?"

"Just for being you."

He stole another quick kiss, "What can I say? I've grown quite partial to my partner." Ennis pushed himself to his feet then hooked his hands beneath her arms, "Come on, Tiger. Let's get you to the hospital."

Bracing herself on the railing, she flinched at the pain now making a strong comeback all over, especially her wounded leg, "Tiger, huh? Before long, you'll know *all* my secrets."

Ennis draped his jacket around her shoulders and offered a sly wink, "You have no idea."

Even through the satisfying warmth of his coat, wariness seasoned her pained look, "What'd Georgia do now? Show you my naked baby pictures?"

"Not exactly," was the cryptic reply. With one arm around her waist, Ennis eased her closer, reminding her to rely on his strength. The mention of babies hammered reality home. The horrific fact resurfaced – according to Terence, he'd sexually molested Lindsey. Being a cop, she'd seen plenty of molested children, and had to literally pull them from the abuser's grasp. She'd dealt with the crime the only way she knew how. She tried to detach. After her shift she'd run the perimeter of Piedmont Park until she literally gave out – until the images faded to a transparency that allowed her to sleep at night. Now, though... Now sexual molestation hit closer to home than she'd ever imagined. How did she deal with *that?* How could she live with the fact Terence violated Lindsey for the sole purpose of revenge aimed at his ex-partner? She had to talk to her niece before the nurses, doctors and detectives converged on the terrified child. She had to know from Lindsey herself if Terence abused her.

She limped toward the door with surprising determination.

Ennis held a hand to her stomach, trying to slow her, "Whoa, sugar. Where's the fire?"

"I have to see about Lindsey." Her voice sounded stronger than she felt. The torment of believing Terence violated her niece hit full force now, along with her aches and pains. "I want to see her." Another bout of crying percolated inside. She could barely see through the brimming tears as they neared the roof's doorway.

Ennis stopped much to her displeasure, tenderly swept her tears away, "She's safe – and rather strong-minded like her aunt. When she figured out I was a cop, she ordered me up here for you."

Frustration ruled her brain. Savannah shook her head and started out on her own again, more tears rolling down her cheeks, "You don't understand, Ennis. Terence *did* something to her. He said he did. I have to see her. I have to know she's okay."

In two long strides, Ennis caught up and braced her shoulders. His expression evolved from authoritative to compassionate as the mental and physical exhaustion peaked and broke over. He cradled her to his chest and Savannah welcomed his embrace, the warmth and comfort soaking into her skin and soul. She held to him as she cried, "It's all my fault. He hurt her because of me, because of what I did."

He held her, seemingly realizing she needed to release the stress and fatigue overload. Shushing her, he eased his hand down her hair, and just let her cry. Still burrowed against his chest, her despondent weeping continued until Ennis parted from the embrace, cupped her face in his hands, "Savannah, listen. Before you jump to conclusions, let's go to the hospital. They'll ask her questions and check her out."

"But Terence said he'd –" her voice caught on the word – she couldn't even say it. The mere thought of his actions motivated her to run back to Terence's corpse and do things to it that would appall everyone present. Glancing back in his direction, her blue eyes narrowed at the sight of the bastard's lifeless body. She wanted just five minutes alone with him...

Ennis's strong arms encircled her waist, breaking her daze of contemplated carnage. He nudged her closer, "He could've lied to hurt you. He knew how much Lindsey means to you."

His statement hit a nerve and she regained hope, "You think he lied?"

"It's a distinct possibility. Let's go see her and have you looked at, okay, sweetheart?"

With each step, her muscles set up and the wound oozed blood. Savannah groaned, "Okay." She felt his arm curl around her again and they proceeded on their way. Another question popped into her mind, "How'd you find me? I had to ditch the car at the cemetery."

"You can thank that clever little niece of yours. She flew down to the phone in the lobby and called 911. Since the whole damn department was on the lookout for her, LaVeau and you, it was a no-brainer and they called my cell and told me. I got here 'bout the same time the uniforms did. That's when she told me to get up here and save you."

"She said that?"

"In those exact words. She'd make a great drill sergeant." He squeezed her closer, "Funny in a way, isn't it? You saved Lindsey and she saved you."

Savannah absently nodded. Karma, destiny, fate or luck. Whatever one called it, it didn't reside in her vocabulary. Until now… Maybe there was something to it after all.

To add to her befuddlement, Ennis swung his arm beneath her legs and swept her effortlessly into his arms. She gasped, startled. Countering her defiant features, he shook his head at her imminent lecture. She could make it just fine, she planned to say. On second thought, it felt pretty nice being carried in a man's arms, especially when that man was Ennis Rutherford.

She leaned into him now, grateful for the lift. She soaked in his heat and relaxed in his hold. A sigh slipped out, surprising them both. Savannah swore his chest broadened as he carried her to the stairway with such grace and ease, she could have fallen asleep had she not hurt so badly.

"There's a good girl," he cooed softly. "Never let it be said I'm not chivalrous. I open doors for ladies, seat them at the supper table and give 'em a lift to the hospital when they've been shot, especially if I'm the one who shot 'em."

Savannah chuckled in spite of herself. Leave it Ennis to put a humorous spin on such an emotionally and physically draining night. "You are a true gentleman. You think of everything."

"Except your psycho ex-partner coming after you. Your daddy is the one who remembered him. Between him and Georgia, they had it nailed."

Savannah was surprised her father even remembered Terence but she was grateful he had, "And thanks to you, Terence won't bother anyone again. Let's take the elevator down, partner." Then she turned to him, "Wait. Did you *really* call me 'sweetheart'?"

15

Savannah slowly wavered toward consciousness. The doctor had given her a whopper shot for the pain in her back and head. Whatever was in it, at least it hadn't blanked her memory. She remembered arguing with the doc about being naked from the waist down while he tended her wound. It was a little too close for comfort, having strange male hands touch her there. Of course, she hadn't minded Ennis touching her there, had she? Oh *no*, not at all. She'd give her eye teeth to feel that again – without the gunshot that is. She'd give her eye teeth to have Ennis kiss her again or carry her in his arms. The man not only looked centerfold handsome but could kiss a woman to her knees.

The doctor wasn't exactly from the canine family either. She guessed his age at about thirty, like her, and to his credit he was a fine looking man, like a living Roman statue, and well built in all the right places, damn him. No wonder she kept yanking at the sheet to cover herself. Ladies didn't just let it all hang out, she'd said, no matter whether the wound was a scratch or spurting arterial blood.

Besides arguing with the doc about being in her altogethers, she also recalled insisting to know about Lindsey. So much so that he'd summoned Georgia to calm her down or shut her up. That's when she discovered Ennis either knew more than he said, or he possessed a dandy sixth sense. According to Georgia, Lindsey was fine and had no signs of sexual abuse. For the first time in her existence, Savannah basically collapsed which allowed the doctor – much to his delight – to work on her wound.

Her eyes opened to a softly lit room – the sun began setting through the taupe curtain across the way – which told her she'd slept for the better part of the day.

Glancing gradually around – for glancing *quickly* encouraged dizziness – she caught sight of her sister's graceful frame folded in a leisure chair positioned beside the bed. Covered in a Pepto Bismol colored blanket, Georgia slept, one elbow on the armrest, her head resting in her palm.

An odd noise shifted Savannah's attention to the right. She blinked to clear her vision. What she saw amazed her. Slumped in a chair, legs splayed out and covered with his own pink blanket sat Ennis Rutherford, snoring up a storm. It began as slow, deep breathing then settled into a rhythmic seesaw of rumbling and sighing.

Savannah smiled at the image. Ennis looked like a boy covered up to his chin and his feet sticking out the bottom of the blanket.

"Good morning – or evening, really," was the whisper from her left. Georgia was awake.

Savannah turned to see her shake the pain out of her wrist. Savannah grimaced, dealing with her own soreness, and settled for, "Mornin'." She liked to think of it as a new day, at least.

The eldest leaned forward in the chair, "How're you feeling?"

"Sore," she whispered back. Then looked over at Ennis again, "How long has he been here?"

"All day." Georgia brushed her fingers through her tousled hair to bring some order to it. "He refused to leave."

A tiny smile curved her lips. *Well, I'll be...* She wanted to wake him, to let him know she was okay but after watching him sleep, decided he not only needed the rest but looked damned endearing in that position.

Georgia continued, "He led your doctor to believe there's more to your partnership than badges."

Briefly returning her gaze to her sister, Savannah observed a shrewd grin spreading like wildfire on her face. Georgia couldn't stand it any longer, "So is there?"

She felt her brow lift, wondering the same. Ennis tended to protect her and yes, they kissed. Oh boy, did they *kiss...* No man in existence managed to kiss her into submission about anything. Ennis, with one memorable lip-lock, convinced her to not only dry her tears but allow him to carry her to the ambulance and ride to the hospital with her. Warning bells instantly clanged in her head. If he was *that* good, she'd really have to be careful or she'd agree to fly to Vegas for a whirlwind marriage...

"I'll take your blush as a 'yes'."

"He's a good kisser," she mumbled, or so she thought.

Georgia chuckled, "He said the same about you."

The comment brought her more awake and she moved,

stretching. Then she regretted it, "I'm so sore even my toenails hurt."

"Doctor says it'll take a while to wear off. For the interim, all you're allowed to do is breathe."

Even through a mask of pain, Savannah answered, "And even that seems pretty laborious right now."

"Stop moving and you won't hurt so much," Georgia directed in a manner reminding Savannah of their mother. "If you remember, the doctor stitched up your wound."

Oh... She did remember that, yes... Vaguely, though. Savannah glanced at Ennis again then back to her sister, "You know, I'm getting more holes in me than a politician's credentials."

With a warning glance, Georgia shushed her, "He already feels like dirt for grazing you with the shot. He's afraid you'll never forgive him."

Savannah noticed the emphasis on "grazing". Well, grazing hurt pretty bad too. Maybe not as bad as a through and through but damn, this was no party either. She wasn't so silly as to blame Ennis – he did what he had to do. She was just grateful he was there to save her. Her vision settled on Georgia, "The bullet didn't hit my brain. I know he did what was required to save me and I'm thankful for it. It's better than the alternative." Now she watched the sleeping man unconsciously readjust his blanket under his chin. Her voice dropped to a whisper, "I'll find a way to thank him."

"You're smiling," Georgia leaned nearer to see the grin on her sister's face. "Savannah Charlene, you are too sore to entertain those type thoughts right now."

She turned back to her older sister, "You're presumptuous, aren't you?" Surprisingly, she hadn't been thinking too seriously along those lines. After all, the quickest way to spoil a great partnership was to sleep together. She had, however, been thinking about having him over for dinner, maybe a movie and, well, they'd wing it at that point. Okay, so the thought *had* crossed her mind, if even briefly...

Georgia retained her knowing expression, but one eyebrow hiked higher than the other, "I raised you, honey. I can read your mind and the signals are telling me Ennis needs to steal all the sleep he can get before you're able to walk right."

"Which should be about next June," she cringed when her stomach rumbled. *Great. Another pain to deal with.* "Know what sounds good right now? I woke up with a powerful hankering for spareribs and one of your peach pies. Corn fritters, fried okra and potatoes and a cucumber sandwich."

Georgia gave her a glance of utter disbelief, "Are you healing or pregnant?"

"It's a miracle if I'm pregnant so it must be the healing thing. Can you swing that for me? Or at least half of it?" Savannah knew she rarely asked for spareribs but the peach pie no one could tear her away from. Georgia once remarked that Savannah sounded downright sexual when talking about the thing and laughed when her sister replied with, "It's so good it'll make you hurt yourself." Or others, for that matter, if they wandered too close to it... Eventually Georgia began making two pies at the holidays, one for the celebration and one specifically for her.

Georgia nodded, "I can arrange it all, no problem. But let's not eat all of that at once. I'd hate to see you turn green at two in the morning."

Savannah grinned. She reveled in the feeling of a genuine smile now. After the ordeal and the sheer panic about Lindsey, she learned to value such small things.

Georgia's voice dropped to a whisper, "I think Ennis is planning to suggest something interesting, to see if you'll agree to do it."

The smile wavered between thoughts of his kisses and other, more serious matters. Unsure whether to keep the grin or ditch it, Savannah replied, "At present I'm not prepared for much so I hope it's not life changing."

Leaning forward in the seat, her sister clearly debated whether to reveal the secret or not. She decided to spill it, "I know how you react to certain proposals –"

"Okay, can you please not use the word *proposal?* Gives me hives." Indeed, she began scratching her arm then her leg at the mention of the word.

"*Proposition* then, does that work? He wants you to meet his family."

Savannah felt paralyzed. Her tongue seized inside her mouth but her eyes widened to dinner plates. Georgia tried to allay her fears, "What's the problem? He's met your family, even some of the more unstable ones. Any man who can withstand the Prince lunacy is worth hanging on to."

Well, she couldn't argue with that. But she didn't like the way her sister phrased it. It sounded domesticated. It sounded like friggin' wedding bells. "Uh, why am I meeting his family if it's not serious? His family is in *Texas*, not down the road in Macon. It's over a thousand miles, Georgia. A thousand miles signifies serious."

Rolling her eyes, Georgia sighed. "Ennis never said he was proposing. He wanted you to decompress from this situation yesterday. He thought getting away from here might help. If you want to panic and put gold rings and groomsmen into the picture, that's your mistake."

"Yeah well, Mama always said I was slow but she never said I was stupid." Charlene never uttered such words but Savannah thought Georgia needed a wake up call. Being the youngest sibling didn't automatically crown her as dense. Somebody – with the name Georgia – was cooking something up and it smelled overdone. Her sister prided herself on knowing Savannah's thoughts – evidently Georgia forgot her younger sister knew hers as well. At the current time, Georgia virtually popped with anticipation. Picking up on certain terminology, Savannah guessed her sister was two steps away from calling a preacher. That concerned her as to what all was discussed the night before while she was on Terence's bizarre journey. Had Ennis declared marriage-minded feelings to Georgia? Or had her sister misunderstood something he'd said?

Savannah's vision returned to the sleeping man in the chair. He might not have mentioned marriage but if she agreed to this trip, she figured his family sure would. On the other hand, taking a small vacation sounded good. She'd dodged Cupid's arrows before when shot from the guy's family so she could handle them. Her big problem was the longer she thought about it, she realized she couldn't remember when her last real vacation was. But Texas? God sakes, what a change that would be...

"You know," Georgia began with a chuckle, "you're Grandma Culberson in the making. That's how I imagine you in your old age."

Savannah turned to oppose that statement but spun too fast and groaned at the soreness, "Take that back or I'll whine you to death." Grandma wasn't a bad person, just a little scary if a person didn't know her. With her at all times was a small Smith & Wesson revolver. She kept it in her apron when she prepared dinner, tucked it in her overalls when she gardened and laid it in her lap when she drank her iced tea.

Grandma maintained she carried the weapon because there were men sitting in the trees above the house and occasionally one would get bold enough to jump down onto the roof and scare the daylights out of her. Savannah recalled one time drinking a glass of iced tea with Grandma when the older woman broke from their conversation to daintily dab the corners of her mouth – with a cloth napkin, of course – and stated, "Think I finally got one of 'em last night." She pointed to a hole in the ceiling, "Heard him scream."

Savannah didn't require a lesson in dealing with Grandma Culberson. Eccentric but lovable as a teddy bear, Grandma didn't pose a threat to family or friends – just the men in the trees. "Good for you, Grandma. I hope you made believers outta all of 'em."

A satisfied smile spread across her gentle face, "Oh, I did, honey. I did."

Breaking from the memory, Savannah chuckled. Grandma's antics certainly created some interesting conversations. Then she thought how funny it *wouldn't* be if, years from now, Lindsey and Dylan found her on her porch with a Smith & Wesson revolver in *her* lap. She tried to shake off the thought and again groaned at the pain rolling through her body, "So when do I go to Texas?"

Georgia shrugged, "I'll ask him. He's finally awake."

Swiveling her vision to Ennis, she watched his legs stretch long and wide beneath the blanket while his arms reached high above his head. He blinked a couple of times to clear his sight then yawned. Mid-yawn he caught the image of both sisters staring at him and smiled tiredly and waved, "Mornin', ladies."

"Mornin'," they replied in unison. Savannah tilted slightly to view Ennis's hair. It stood straight up at the back and fanned out like a brown peacock's tail. She pointed to him then her hair. He looked in the mirror, his jaw dropped at the sight. Sliding a comb from his back pocket he worked with his hair until he looked presentable. He smiled at Savannah in the mirror and mouthed a "thank you".

Georgia stood to fold her blanket, "So Ennis, when are you taking Savannah to meet your family?"

Good thing Savannah wasn't drinking or eating at the time or she'd have spewed. Her partner also showed signs of shell-shock. He glanced at her then back at Georgia whose brow lifted in expectation of an answer. "Um, well," he stammered.

"Georgia, that's unfair," Savannah complained. "Ambushing him after he just woke up."

Ennis waved off the comment, "No, no. I'm awake, believe me. That question was better than a rooster crowing in my ear." He paused momentarily then blurted, "How 'bout after Thanksgiving? Think you'll be mobile by then?"

Wanting to hit him but only with something soft, Savannah tried reaching for Georgia's pillow then fussed when her sister slapped her hand away. She sighed, "I'm thirty, Ennis, not a hundred and thirty. I'll be ready."

"Really?" His stunned features met Georgia who winked. He obviously still couldn't believe it, "You'll go?"

The nod was tentative, "Georgia told me you wanted me to meet your family."

"I do."

Okay, maybe the previous night's chasing scrambled her brains, but why did everything everyone said sound connected to marriage? She hoped it wasn't *her* having the thoughts of matrimony. She seemed strangely preoccupied with the notion. She pinched herself to make sure she felt the same about nuptials as before. Yep, all systems up and operational. Marriage was a no-go. A veritable ball and chain, that's exactly what exchanging vows symbolized.

Savannah found herself relaxing now. She shrugged at her partner, "Well, then we'd better make plans as to where I'm staying." She teased, "They got hotels in Texas?"

This time Ennis balked in utter disbelief, "You're joking. My mama raised a gentleman. You stay at the ranch with me and the whole Hee Haw gang, sweetheart."

"There you go again calling me sweetheart," she replied lightheartedly. "Are we going steady or what? And another thing.

Speaking of Hee Haw, does your family have a penchant for singing that annoying song like you do?"

Confused, Georgia inquired, "What song?"

Ennis grinned like a fool then chuckled, "I torment her occasionally with the thing. Of course, she's pretty enough she knows I'm kidding her."

Savannah harrumphed but allowed her smile to broaden. Oh yes, the trip to Texas would be wild and wooly. Allowing herself to time trip forward, she could already hear the resonant singing drifting from a ranch house in the middle of nowhere. Just from the tune and lyrics, the more she recognized the place as the Rutherford Ranch. As she neared the house, each Rutherford stood tall and sang proudly and loudly like an old-fashioned Baptist tent revival...

"Where oh where are you tonight?
Why did you leave me here all alone?
I searched the world over and I thought I'd found true love.
But you met another and PFFT! You was gone.

You took out your false teeth, your wig and your glasses.
You were just scattered all over the place.
I wanted to kiss you and hug you so tightly.
I guess that I would have if I'd found your face.

I went to your house at three in the morning.
You had all them curlers and junk in your hair.

You would not have scared me and I'd not have run so,

If you had not looked like you'd wrestled a bear.

I told you my darlin' you looked like a gopher.

Made you so mad, you haven't spoke since.

But tell me my darling if you ain't got buck teeth.

How do you eat apples through a picket fence?"

Oh my God, Savannah wondered.   *What have I just agreed to?*

J.L. Lemon lives in Texas surrounded by a loving and supportive family, two adorable and devoted puppies, and hordes of garden gnomes.

Savannah and Ennis keep the author busy taking dictation and making plenty of suggestions about their future.

www.ingramcontent.com/pod-product-compliance
Lightning Source LLC
Chambersburg PA
CBHW020600250626
47154CB00004B/1301